NO CHOICE BUT DEATH

"Did you find the girls?" Ian questioned.

"Yes, two. Did you?" Rebecca replied.

"Only one."

"The second girl I located was Hester," Rebecca told him happily. "Now, give me a hand, will you?"

Together they carried the body of the senseless Paiute back into the rocks to a place beyond hearing from the village. By then, the y... ad begun to come around. Roughly, they ... burden.

"Do you spea... slowly.

"Little ... n."

"Wha...

"*Kwin*... e go away like storm in ...

Rebecca ... attempt at interrogation with little succes...

"There's nothing more we can get out of him," the white squaw said with finality.

"You'll turn him loose, then?" Ian asked.

"And have all those Paiute warriors on our backs before we can get out of this canyon? No. I don't like it, but we're going to have to kill him."

Shocked, the reverend stared a long moment. "I can't quite adjust to the idea of such a cold-blooded act," he protested.

With a sigh of regret, Rebecca drew her knife, bent down and drove its sharp blade into the frightened, wide-eyes Paiute's heart. When she withdrew it, a gush of warm crimson flooded over her hand and forearm. For a moment she felt her stomach churn and lurch. Then she remembered Roger Styles and what he liked to do to little girls—and what he had done to her.

"I'm sorry, Ian. It was necessary. We'd better get away from here fast."

WHITE SQUAW
Zebra's Adult Western Series
by E.J. Hunter

Available wherever paperbacks are sold, or order direct from the Publisher. Send cover price plus 50¢ per copy for mailing and handling to Zebra Books, Dept. 1882, 475 Park Avenue South, New York, N.Y. 10016. Residents of New York, New Jersey and Pennsylvania must include sales tax. DO NOT SEND CASH.

#11 HOT-HANDED HEATHEN

BY E J HUNTER

ZEBRA BOOKS
KENSINGTON PUBLISHING CORP.

Special acknowledgments to Mark K. Roberts

ZEBRA BOOKS

are published by

Kensington Publishing Corp.
475 Park Avenue South
New York, NY 10016

First printing: August 1986

Printed in the United States of America

This volume of Rebecca Caldwell's adventures is dedicated to a good friend and faithful reader: Dr. Patricia Cummins.

— EJH

"Although long exposed to the civilizing efforts of the Church, the Mexican Government, and the Spanish before them, the Yuma, Pima, and Paiute tribes frequently took, and held, white women captives."
—*Desert Dwellers of the Southwest*
J. R. Hudson

Chapter 1

With the Great Salt Flats safely passed, nothing bad could possibly happen, Joel Benchley thought with relief. With Josh and the Cap'n ahead on a long scout, life could be mighty easy. He scratched idly in his wiry, salt-and-pepper beard and surveyed the pastel-hued strata of the spindly rock spires that dotted the land. Their varied colors had been laid bare over countless years by the incessant winds of northern Nevada Territory. From his position at the head of the long column of wagons, he could see far into the distance ahead and to both sides. Yep, he repeated to himself, nothing could go wrong now.

Then the Paiutes attacked.

Bronze-skinned warriors rose from among the gullies and rust-colored boulders and loosed a flight of arrows. Some struck the rumps of draft animals, causing them to whinny or bray pitifully in their agony. Other projectiles thudded into the high, wooden sides of Conestogas and freight wagons. A few found targets in flesh.

"Open 'em up!" Joel shouted. "Injuns! Give yer critters their heads."

Ponderously at first, the heavy-laden vehicles re-

9

sponded. More feathered missiles moaned through the air. Women and children of the immigrant families cried out in fright and hardened teamsters cursed. Several among the fleeing whites reached for their weapons, while here and there the long shafts of war lances wobbled erratically toward their targets. A man pitched forward, under the hoofs of his wheelers. The reins were picked up by his horror-stricken wife. A few random shots from the Paiute attackers blasted through the dusty air. Then the worst thing Joel could expect happened.

More Indians appeared, a double file, mounted on sturdy, galloping horses. Their shrill war cries sounded over the rumble of pounding hoofs and the groaning protest of the wagons. The Paiute warriors swept in toward both sides of the fleeing column.

"Circle up," Joel shouted desperately. "Circle the wagons!"

Long practice insured quick response to his order. The lead wagon slowed slightly and its driver guided the six-up team to the right. Pivoting on almost the exact spot, those behind followed suit. Clouds of gritty dust boiled around the bending arc of wagons.

To Joel's experienced eyes, the circle formed with agonizing slowness. Festoons of arrows grimly decorated most of the lumbering vehicles. In contrast the Paiutes closed in with terrible swiftness.

Kwina-Pagunupa looked on with satisfaction. The powerful medicine given him by *Tazinupa* worked well. The foolish whites fled before his warriors like rabbits. Only a few attempted to fight. Their bullets had no effect. Truly, his warriors were immune to the flying lead. Eagle Cloud carefully judged the time, then raised a feathered hoop in a signal. He and his horsemen rode out of hiding in a low gully and split into two ranks, to stream down the sides of the column of wagons. Yes, he thought again, Star's medicine had a true magic about it.

"Don't let them circle," he shouted to his followers. "Cut the wagons off. You cannot be hurt. My medicine is strong. We will kill them all and take their horses."

Slowly the long string began to bend, then to turn in on itself. The whites formed a circle. No matter, Eagle Cloud dismissed it. A bullet cracked past his head. See, he told himself. The magic of *Tazinupa* was strong. Let the pale ones stop running. All the easier to kill them then.

"Strike hard! Strike hard, my brothers!" he yelled in encouragement.

"See," Weather Bird called to him. "They form a turtle. This will be easy."

The Reverend Ian Claymore watched the onslaught of the Paiute warriors and offered up a prayer for the safety of the wagon train. Then he reached one arm back in the wagon for his fine quality, long-barreled Parker shotgun. The twelve-gauge had been the only luxury he had indulged in after his ordination, his Kentucky hill-country upbringing calling strongly to him each fall, when a plethora of pigeons, grouse, and turkeys summoned him into the field to hunt.

Ian didn't consider it incongruous for a minister of the gospel to be an avid tracker and harvester of game. Quite to the contrary. The land abounded with enormous surpluses of edible animals. And in Genesis, it said that God had filled the seas with fishes and the land with animals and that man had dominion over all. That man took of the fields and the seas and feasted and all was well in God's world. So, why not in this new

11

land, so far from that described in Biblical times? Right then, the shotgun felt a great comfort to him.

He laid the richly engraved barrels of the Parker across his lap and hauled hard on the right reins. A few more yards and the circle would be complete, he estimated. A bronze body loomed in close to the wagon. Claymore looped the reins around his left thigh and raised the shotgun. One barrel boomed loudly and coughed up a gout of greasy smoke.

Buckshot pellets sped ahead of the flame and cloud. They ripped into the chest of a Paiute warrior and sent him hurtling from his horse's back. Almost at once, another took his place. Ian Claymore fired again.

"Good shootin', Reveren'," Joel Benchly called to him from the opposite side of the careening wagon. "Haul in on 'em and and let's close the circle."

The six-foot-three blond giant nodded and exerted the strength of his powerful arms to draw his six-up of mules to a slow walk. "Woah, Ned, ho-up, Nellie. Easy now, Sam," he soothed with the accomplished skill of an experienced mule skinner. "Haw! Haw! Woah-up!"

"Ian . . . Ian," a timorous voice quavered from inside the canvas-covered wagon. "Is it . . . have they . . . ?"

"We've stopped the wagons," Claymore told his six-teen-year-old sister. "It's better for defense, Hester. You keep down, under the goose-down covers. Don't come out unless I call you."

Dark blue eyes, large with fear, wide-set and surrounded by thick, sable lashes, blinked at him, then disappeared as the creamy-complexioned young woman dodged back inside the bed. A tightness formed in Ian's throat. His sister was the only living relative who tied him to family or home. God protect her, he prayed silently. An arrow thudded into the side of his wagon as the team came to a stop.

"Everybody down, behind your wagons," Joel Benchley bawled. "Take yer time, aim good, and squee-eeze off. Them Injuns think more of their horses than themselves. Shoot their mounts out from under 'em an' they's helpless. More or less," he added in a quieter tone.

"They'll be coming soon," Claymore observed.

"You fought Injuns before, Rev'ran'?"

"No, Mr. Benchley. But at home in the Kentucky hills, I heard many a story about the Creek, the Choctaw, and the Natchez. And about my distant cousin, Boone."

Joel cocked an eye. "Ol' Dan'el?"

"The same, only so distant he'd not likely claim me as kin," Ian added modestly. "I hate shooting horses. It's not their fault."

"Just so. But in this case, they're just like any other infernal machine. They're bein' used as a means of bringin' war to us. Look lively, Rev'ran', and don't be firin' that scattergun until the heathens' are well in range."

Ian let his smile expand into a chuckle. "I don't figure there'll be any problem with that. Our attackers would have to pull off a bit, as it is now, to be where I can't reach them with this Parker."

"Parker, eh?" Joel asked with genuine appreciation. "English gun, ain't it? One of the best."

"My one concession to vanity and worldly gains. It cost a goodly sum, though it'll last more than one lifetime."

"Make every one of 'em count. I've got to move along, see to the others."

Behind the wagon scout, Ian took aim on a lean, muscular Paiute who appeared to be directing the others. The squat, compact body moved with an energy that radiated power. Dressed in a colorful breastplate of what appeared to be thick Italian brocade, the colors bright and gaudy, the fierce-faced warrior waved a hoop-shaped device around to dispatch his followers to assigned positions. The loop, set atop a slender rod had been decorated with beads and feathers. Several eagle-wing pinions dangled from long strips of rawhide. Ian centered the front bead sight on the Indian's chest and squeezed gently.

The Parker roared and bucked. Smoke obscured Ian's vision, but he knew that at the range, he could not have missed. When the wind whisked away the curtain of powder grime, Ian blinked, unable to believe what he saw.

He couldn't have missed! Not at less than twenty yards. Yet, if any pellets had struck the howling savage, they must have bounced off. Impossible. Surely the padded breastplate could not have stopped the heavy lead balls. Worried, his curiosity aroused over the cold feeling in his gut, Ian fired the second barrel. He dodged to the side this time to see the effect.

Nothing. Bits of brocade flew from the front of the leader's chest protector, and he rocked back in the saddle from obvious impact. Incredibly, the man kept his seat. No blood showed. He hurled an angry, yet contemptuous glare at Ian and kicked his pony's ribs. He raised his hoop contraption and hooted noisily. With a wave toward a distant, lone cactus, he streaked across the dusty ground in that direction.

Instantly, the ululating braves followed him.

"They're massing for an attack," Joel advised everyone. "Hold steady. Wait for 'em to come up to ya. Then blast 'em inta Hell . . . uh, pardon, Rev'ran'."

"No need for pardon, Mr. Benchley. The way I see it, the Lord knows His own. We kill 'em and we let God sort 'em out."

Benchley spit a long stream of tobacco juice and

14

slapped a palm on the inside of his left thigh. "By jingoes, that shines! You heard the parson, folks — open season on savages. Let the fur fly!"

Moments later, the Paiutes came. In repeated waves of fifteen to twenty warriors, the howling braves plunged down to the circled caravan. Careful, level-headed marksmanship turned the first assault. Three Paiute fighting men died, several received wounds. Eleven horses whinnied and tumbled into the dirt to kick out their lives. Not bad, Joel Benchley considered.

Even as he noted the Paiute losses, he made a quick calculation as to the strength of those remaining. Only too damned good, he conceded. Hoofs pounding like the surf of the distant Pacific, the Paiutes charged again. A man close to the scout reared back as blood flew from his shuttered head.

Benchley took aim on the murderous savage who had killed the teamster. He spat out a squirt of brown-tinged saliva and squeezed off a round.

A hot 205-grain hung of lead split the breastbone of the Paiute and sent him backward over his pony's rump. Good. One less of the bastards.

Eagle Cloud watched his men die without the least trepidation. They had not believed, or they would not die. His own special medicine, an ancient plate of low-grade steel, pounded into rough shape to fit his barrel chest, protected him. For his followers, faith alone provided the shield. Better now to weed out the weak and the unbelievers, before the big war began to drive all the whites from Paiute land. His must be the true deliverance. Not just the first, but the one that would truly lead the way. Already there was talk of another who worked great medicine.

Among the Snakes to the east, so it was said, a

young boy had begun to mystify his elders and the medicine men of the tribe. Wovoka, but a child not yet past puberty, saw visions and spoke of a time when the buffalo would come back and the whites would be driven forever from the land. *Kwina-Pagunupa* knew that it would not wait for Wovoka to complete his vision, not wait for him to reach the mature years of a man. Let the boy dream. He, Eagle Cloud, would triumph. It would start here, with this traveling village of whites.

The next charge would do it, he figured. His men would breach the defenses at the weak points between wagons. Then the slaughter could commence in style. He found it hard to wait. He had seen many children there: Boys to be adopted into the tribe; girls to be used for pleasure, made into camp slaves, and eventually discarded like used-up buffalo-paunch kettles. Heeaaah-haa! That was the way. Now. Send the final wave of warriors.

Blood splashed through the air in torrents. Men and women screamed and died; arrows, lances, and tomahawks ripping at their flesh. Paiutes died, too, wondering at the failure of their leader's promises. Had they lacked enough faith? When the glut of slaughter ended and the looting began, the Paiutes exhibited a ferocity beyond that of warriors seeking revenge on their enemy.

They tore dresses from the dead women and mutilated their bodies. The wounded shrieked horribly while the maddened braves tortured them, then gave the men merciless ends by forcing them to swallow fire or have their genitals cut off so that they bled to death. The women they raped, before visiting similar indignities on their abused bodies. Children, horrified and in

16

semiconscious states of shock, wailed and moaned. So excited did the victorious Paiutes become, they failed to hear the approach of several persons.

Shots crackled from the rifles of a dozen white men. Surprised, on foot and away from their well-trained war ponies, the Paiutes panicked and took flight. They ran in confusion for a while, allowing the whites to kill several of their number. Then the warriors mounted and rode off, taking along their human prizes to add to the population of their camp.

"Well, Brothers," a tall, lean man with a mean face and long slash scar on his right cheek inquired. "What is your pleasure?"

"What is the will of the One, Brother Thackery?" a dour, horse-faced individual countered.

"Obviously, He saw fit to have the Paiutes get here too far ahead of us. There are few here of worth or interest to us. Let those who can survive. For the rest, leave them."

"Aye. That's a fair way to decide it, Brother Thackery."

Despite the pitiful moans of the few survivors and the muted cursing of Joel Benchley, the austere men in their dark suits and black, dome-crowned, flat-brim hats rode off into the desert. Their dust lingered a long while, accompanied by lamentations from those desperately abandoned by their own kind.

Chapter 2

Bursting with a startling array of pale yellows, ambers, reds, purples, browns, Fall had come to the Wallowa Valley of Oregon. Here and there, like sturdy sentinels of springtime, the evergreen of firs and pines, a few stubborn alders and beeches, remained for contrast. The birds had taken on their somber plumage of winter and the scampering rabbits had already begun to thicken and lighten their coats in preparation for heavy snow cover. A lithe, graceful young woman and a tall, muscular young man rode out of the valley, hearts heavy with regret at departing from so much beauty.

Rebecca Caldwell had made her farewells to *Hinmah-toyahlet-keht*, known to the whites as Chief Joseph, and had seen to the packing of the many gifts that had been pressed upon her for what she had accomplished in saving the Nez Percé's spotted-rump horses. She was mounted upon one of the magnificent beasts, leading three more. At her side rode her companion of many months.

Although he preferred to go by the name Lone Wolf, which he had won during captivity among the Crow, Brett Baylor could easily, if not comfortably, assume the persona of his former white life when circumstances dictated. Lean and hard from his life as an Absaroka warrior, Lone Wolf had a classic handsomeness that wore any clothes with style. His blond hair contrasted markedly with the nearly blue-black of Rebecca's. Both had known life among the Indians and each, for personal reasons, preferred to emulate much they had learned. Baylor traveled in buckskins, Rebecca in elk hide, done in the fashion of her Oglala Sioux relatives. Except for where they encountered traditional enemies of their tribes, the garb served as badges of safe conduct and opened the portals of hospitality. They traveled southward now, toward the remaining open passes to California. In particular, Rebecca sought the fabled Mormon Road to San Diego.

Some guiding hunch told her that she would find Roger Styles again if she journeyed to that growing community on the sheltered bay. That she wanted a great deal. She had lost track of exactly how long she had hunted Roger. Only, lately, she had begun to feel more like the pursued than the pursuer. More to convince herself than her companion, she spoke aloud of it again as their mounts strained into the upslope of the Humboldt Range foothills.

"Where else could Roger have gone?" Rebecca inquired rhetorically. "He's wanted in Oregon now. Washington Territory is too close and everyone knows everyone else. It has to be California, and the further south, the safer. That's how Roger would think."

"He could always go back East. Leave the frontier," Lone Wolf suggested.

"I don't think so. Oh, he likes his luxury and so on. That's why I settled on California. Who knows how many crimes Roger is wanted for now? At least all the way to the Mississippi. The real East, beyond there to

19

the Atlantic, is too settled for Roger to feel comfortable. There's too much law and order for a man like him to operate."

Lone Wolf gave her a cynical grin. "Unless he entered politics. He tried that before, in Colorado, remember? Nearly won a seat in the newly forming state legislature, representing his own town of Grubstake."

"How well I recall that," Rebecca answered tightly. "I nearly became a slave to opium, thanks to him. Somehow I think that was worse than . . . all the other things."

White mantles capped the higher peaks and the wind blowing off them carried a hoary breath that presaged the coming winter. Time seemed suspended as the pair rode ever higher into the mountains. Spectacular waterfalls generated pleasant excitement in Rebecca and she spoke often to Lone Wolf of the quantity and variety of wildlife.

Grouse, quail, and a wide assortment of smaller, edible birds abounded. Fish jumped in the crystal streams. Deer and elk moved in lazy herds, grazing without noticeable worry about predators, though wolves howled from close and far during the nights when the pair camped. Lone Wolf shot a sturdy elk calf and they feasted for three days on its succulent meat, preserved by the coolness of the air. Once over the crest, the pace of their journey increased.

"Did you notice how different the Nez Percé are from the tribes we're familiar with?" Rebecca inquired one afternoon, after a week on the trail.

"How do you mean?"

"They can fight, and well. No question of that. But they lead a settled, more peaceful life than the Sioux or Crow. For all that, they have horses."

Lone Wolf shrugged. "This country . . . it makes a

person feel lazy. Who wants to work up all the enthusiasm and spend the energy to wander and raid other tribes when all's needed to live a good life is a salmon scoop or an hour in the woods to bag a deer or elk?"

"Hummm. You may have a point. It got to where I would rather spend my day doing simple jobs around the village instead of riding off looking for something."

"Even Roger's rustlers?" Lone Wolf teased.

"That's not fair. Of course I wanted to stop them. Only . . . somehow, taken day by day, nothing seemed all that urgent. Now, if it had been Iron Calf . . ."

Images crowded Rebecca's mind as she saw again the bustling village of her natural father, Iron Calf of the Oglala . . ."

"Ho! A stranger comes . . . a stranger comes!" the *Eyanpaha* of Iron Calf's village cried out as he rode his pony, decorated with the symbols of his office, around the hoops of the village.

A clutch of nervousness gripped at Rebecca Caldwell's middle. Strangers nearly always meant trouble. In her second year of living with Iron Calf's band, Rebecca had eyes and thoughts for only one person — Four Horns, the handsome, supple youth of eighteen summers, who had but two months earlier introduced her to the delicious thrills of lovemaking. Even as she watched the stately approach of the stranger, a good-looking young Cheyenne warrior, she grew moist in her secret place and tingled in anticipation of her next opportunity to thrill herself and Four Horns with the revels of fleshly celebration. They had planned for it to be this night. Down on the creek bank.

Oh, please, she thought desperately, don't let this stranger coming keep us from being together tonight. Barely past her sixteenth birthday, Rebecca's deflowering by Four Horns had swung wide the portals to a rich, pervasive sensuality that seemingly knew no bounds.

Before he had come into her life, things had been far different. The sexual satisfaction she experienced, from a variety of self-stimulating techniques, had seemed the ultimate joy. But then had come the shattering change in her life.

Traded off, along with her mother, to Iron Calf and his Oglala braves in exchange for freedom for a band of outlaws, she had been little more than a slave for a year. When her stubbornness receded, she won better acceptance by the girls of the village. Another year had passed. However, the fate generally reserved for female captives did not touch her. She had remained, technically, a virgin. Until Four Horns came along.

An encounter at the bathing spot along the creek left her thrilled to the queasy point by the firm pressure of his rigid maleness pressing against her naked belly. They had arranged a risky meeting for that night and she had trembled with anxiety and anticipation until he slipped under the skirt of the small lodge next to Iron Calf's, where she slept. With tender care he had guided her to new peaks of delight, then brought about the fulfillment of her promise as a woman. Nothing, nothing, she swore, could ever be quite like it.

Her thinking had not changed on that point. Eagerly she followed along to the wide space before Iron Calf's lodge. The visitor made his purpose known in a loud voice.

"The *Pani* are dancing to the sacred drum. They are mixing paint and making ready for war. Men of the Blackfoot people have been among them stirring up hatred against my people and yours. There'll be raids before the fat-moon berries ripen. I was sent to warn your people, others go to the different bands of the Dakota."

"The *Sahiela* are our cousins," Iron Calf spoke slowly. "It's good you come with this message. How do our cousins choose?"

"We will fight. The battle is to be taken to the *Pani* before they can make ready."

"Then the warriors of this band will ride with you." Iron Calf turned to the gathering throng of Oglala. "Who among you will take up the pipe of war? Who leads for the Red Top Oglala?"

A chorus of "I's" followed. Iron Calf nodded in satisfaction. His shrewd eyes twinkled as he contemplated the choices. At last he gestured with his chin, in the polite manner, to indicate Runs Backward.

"Here is a war leader of many seasons. Will he take up the sacred pipe? Here is a person wise in the ways of the warpath. Who would go with him? Here is a person who brings back those who follow the pipe in his hands. Who would go with him? Here is a person who takes many of the enemy's ponies. Who would go with him? Here is a person who has counted many *coups*. Who would go with him? Here is a person who has taken many scalps. Who would go with him?" The ritual invitation completed, Iron Calf stood with arms folded over his barrel chest and cast a steady gaze on the men of his band.

Runs Backward took two bold steps and placed his hands on the sacred pipe of war that had been brought out by a slender lad of twelve. "I am Runs Backward. All here know me. I take up the sacred pipe of war. Who follows me?"

"I touch the pipe and ride with Runs Backward," Cross-eye declared loudly.

"And I," Broken Horn announced.

"Take me, take me!" two dozen warriors cried out. Some became excited enough to break out in impromptu dances. Others hooted and clapped their hands over their open mouths. A few clasped forearms in a circle and began to shuffle to the left, then back to the right. Rebecca's heart neared to bursting when she saw Four Horns among them. Oh, when would they go? And for how long?

To her immense relief and pleasure, Rebecca got her night with Four Horns. He came to her when the full moon cast silver rays from halfway up the black velvet sky. Except for the herd boys, the villagers slept soundly. She waited in agitation until she heard his step. In a rush they came together on the firm, damp mud of the bank, water lapping at their bare ankles.

Four Horns embraced her and she felt the hard bulk of his lance against her quivery belly. They kissed, long and sweetly.

"I was afraid you wouldn't be here," they said together, and stifled their laughter.

"Oh, Four Horns, hurry. Let's get undressed. I can hardly stand it," Rebecca begged.

Moonbeams burnished their coppery skin as they quickly shed their clothing. Rebecca gasped, as she had the first time she saw the long, fat bulk of his throbbing organ. Eagerly, she reached out for it and enclosed the warm, silky flesh in her pliant fingers.

"Ooooh," Four Horns moaned.

Slowly at first, Rebecca stroked him, working faster and faster. In the silvery light she could see his heart pounding against the taut skin of his broad chest. Her pert breasts swayed and jiggled with the energy of her ministrations and she felt the wild pulsations of her own mounting passion. She sighed and pressed closer to him.

"Over here," she panted. "I found something earlier

that I thought . . ."

"A new game, *Sinaskawin?*" he asked in mock boredom.

"Yes, beloved, a new game. I found this exposed root and I thought . . ."

"What good is it? Tell me how you thought to use it."

"Well, if I bend way over and grasp it, and spread my legs very wide, you can take me like a mighty stallion."

The image inflamed the youthful Oglala. He wet dry lips and nodded. "All right. We — we can try it, I guess."

"Oh, wonderful," Rebecca rejoiced, bending far over.

"Ummmm. What a beautiful sight," Four Horns murmured as he examined the treasure trove exposed to his view by her unorthodox position. Eagerly he stepped closer.

A new burst of thrills coursed through Rebecca's slender figure when the hot tip of Four Horns's engorged staff pressed into her. Great bursts of colored lights went off in both of the lusty teen-agers' heads as he increased his penetration. Rebecca trembled with overwhelming euphoria and feared her knees would give way.

He reached out and grasped her by the hip bones and began a rapid pistoning, in and out, that sent shivers of unexpressable delirium up and down her spine. Rebecca bit her lip and made soft mewing sounds, her head thrashing from side to side as the sensitive flesh of her inner being took tender assault after assault and her mind whirled in absolute sensual overload.

She wanted to cry out her delight for all the world to hear. How could so simple a thing be so magnificent?

"Oh . . . oh . . . don't stop. Don't ever stop. Faster, Four Horns, faster. Make the earth move and the sky dissolve for me."

Eager to oblige, Four Horns plunged onward until both goals had been achieved . . .

Rebecca Caldwell blinked away the vibrant, sensual impressions and wiped a hand across her mouth to remove her dreamy smile. Yes. Life among the Oglala had been decidedly different. And sometimes, so heavenly fulfilling.

"We'd ought to make better time," she suggested, "there's a long way to go."

Lodges scattered haphazardly around the dusty little valley to which the Paiute warriors brought Hester Claymore and three other young women from the wagon train. Women and children ran about the walking captives, shrilly yelling in their faces and spitting at them. One old, toothless crone reached out and viciously pinched Hester's right breast, giving it a nasty twist.

"Wha-what are they going to do to us, Hester?" fourteen-year-old Priscilla Meadows asked in a quavering voice.

"I . . . don't know, Priss. Only it doesn't look good."

At the center of the make-shift encampment, the warriors halted. The leader stepped in front of the captured girls, one hand on his hip, the other holding a braided horsehair whip. His lips curled in disdain and he thrust his chin forward.

"I am called Eagle Cloud," he told the frightened females in heavily accented English. "You belong Paiute now — to do with as we please. First me, then give you to my men."

"What does he mean? *What does he mean?*" Priscilla shrieked in fright, only too sure she knew exactly what he meant.

Kwina-Pagunupa leered at her, the hot light of lust in

26

his eyes. Slowly, with an elaborate gesture, he reached down and squeezed his crotch. Two of his followers grabbed at Priscilla's dress and ripped it away from her body. A chorus of ahs and ohs rose among the spectators as the frightened girl's alabaster skin came into view.

"Take her to my lodge," Eagle Cloud commanded.

"No! Oh, no! Please don't . . . don't do . . . th-th-th . . ." Priscilla shrieked in terror.

Hester Claymore gritted her teeth at the pitiful sight of the hysterical girl and what was about to happen to her. Would they all truly be subject to such a degrading fate? Oh, God, don't let it be, she prayed. A rough Indian hand grabbed her left breast and squeezed it.

"I take you. You be good for much fun."

At least let me faint, Hester pleaded to her deity. Let me not be a part of this filth. The savage who had claimed her leered as he led her roughly away toward another tipi. Inside, he made motions for her to undress.

"I will not."

"Me take, then."

Panther-swift, he lunged at the slender girl and snagged the bodice of her dress. It shredded in long tears down the front. Her petticoats and chemise quickly followed. Shame and humiliation carmined Hester's lithe, peaches-and-cream complexion and she covered her small rosebud-tipped breast with one hand and arm. Defensively, she crossed her legs and tried to conceal her womanly flesh with the other.

A grunting chuckle, much like that of a rooting hog Hester thought, came from the warrior as he stepped closer and pried her hands away. He licked his lips with visceral hunger at the sight of her exposed body and whipped aside his loincloth. He had the largest male member Hester had ever seen, not that she'd had opportunity to observe a great many. Without a word, he threw her to a stack of cured animal hides and dropped his weight atop her.

He smelled awful, Hester thought incongruously. His weight hurt her hips and stomach and mashed her tender breasts. She felt him fumbling around at her waist, fingers probing, prying. Then . . . oh, God, then the pain. Horrible, rasping, burning slivers of agony that threatened to rob her of sanity. Hester's mouth opened, misshapen by torment. She screamed piercingly.

And kept on screaming.

Chapter 3

Scrub pine and stunted alders had begun to give way to desert flora, with the tall spires of yucca, maguey and the skeletal fingers of ocotillo. Still in the western-slope foothills of the Humboldt Range, Rebecca and Lone Wolf caught their first glimpses of the vast, rolling desert that stretched far away to the south and west. Rebecca first spotted a thin smudge on the horizon. "Over there, Lone Wolf. That can't be a campfire this early. Besides, there's too much black in the column of smoke."

"Hummm. You're right. Look there, a little to the left of it. Another one."

"I see it. And another. Someone burning to clear land?"

"Not in a desert. I think we've run into someone else's trouble." Lone Wolf flashed a white smile of large, even teeth.

"We'd better find out."

"Might as well. We're going that way anyway."

An hour's hard ride brought the duo into sight of the blackened remains of five wagons. Three more, partially burned, sat in what was left of a circle, along with six relatively undamaged conveyances. Weary, cautious men, shoulders slumped by defeat, appeared, rifles at the ready.

"It's Injuns!" a small boy's voice piped with a tremor.

"They look white to me," a man's steady voice declared.

"More sight-seers come to gawk?" inquired a grizzled old man with a pronounced stoop and gnarly knuckles caused by arthritis.

"We saw the smoke. We came to see if we could help," Lone Wolf replied.

"Well, now, that's a change, fer dang sure."

"What do you mean?" Rebecca Caldwell inquired.

"There was some folks, a passel of men done up in black suits and funny hats, come by 'bout an hour after the Paiutes hit us. They ran off the ones who stayed to loot, then took off themselves without a by-your-leave, leavin' us stranded here. I'm Joel Benchley, scout and cook for the company. Though I suspect there ain't no more *company*. If the Paiutes didn' ambush Cap'n Long an' Josh before they attacked us, I'm a blue-skinned mule."

"Stands to reason," Rebecca speculated aloud. "I'm Rebecca Caldwell and this is my friend and associate, Brett Baylor. How many of you are left?"

"Better than I expected, Miz Caldwell," Joel replied. "Countin' the wounded, we're near to twenty strong."

"The hostiles stole four girls, including my sister."

Rebecca nearly gasped when the powder-grimed, tall young man stepped forward from the group gathered before her and Lone Wolf. Such beautiful, soft brown eyes! For a moment she became lost in them. A thick shock of blond hair hung carelessly down over his forehead, slanted to the left. He had a calm about him that the others lacked, his broad shoulders straighter, body graceful in movement. In an embarrassed flash, she realized he was still speaking.

"I'm the Reverend Ian Claymore, Miss Caldwell. My sister, Hester, and three other girls were spared being murdered. Some of the Indians rode off earlier on and took them along. Now, I'm a bit more worried about their fate than had they been slain."

"And for good reason," Lone Wolf blurted out tactlessly. "Uh . . . I'm sorry. It's not always that women captives are subjected to tortures. Many are used as slaves, others to fill lodges left empty by death."

"*Married* to the savages?" Claymore asked, paling to the point his freckles stood out markedly on the line of his cheekbones.

"You could call it that, Reverend," Rebecca remarked mildly. "By their own ways, it's a marriage. I should know. For five years, I was a captive of the Oglala Sioux. For three of those, I knew two husbands. I'm sorry for your sister and for you. You've cause to be concerned." She looked around. "You're going to need help getting anywhere from here. We haven't enough horses . . ."

"Some of the stock's bound to stray from the Paiutes," Joel offered. "Especially the mules. Most Injuns don't have any use for them critters. 'Cept to eat. If we can mount a few men on your spares, we can round up a few, I'd say. Half a dozen have already wandered back on their own. We got 'em tethered in that wash over there."

"Good. That's a start," Lone Wolf offered. He exchanged a glance with Rebecca. "All right. We'll do what we can. The first priority is to get you mobile again."

"Then what?" a man of middle height with the florid face of a heavy drinker demanded.

"It would be nice if something could be done about rescuing those girls," Ian Claymore suggested tenta-

31

tively.

"Let's get the draft animals rounded up and fix what wagons can be repaired first, then we can talk about that," Rebecca decided for them. "I sympathize with you," she said to the minister, feeling a powerful tug and a familiar tingling in her loins.

"But without some means of transportation, you'd be helpless to do anything to effect a rescue. Now, those of you who have horses, ride with me, and we'll see how many animals we can find. Brett knows a great deal more about wagons and harness than I do. He'll stay here and help you salvage enough useful vehicles."

"That's right nice of you both," Jim Andrews rumbled in a deep bass. "D'you ever hear of folks like those that ran off on us? Who could do a thing like that?"

"It's not normal," Rebecca agreed. "Not out in country like this. Now, if it were further east, I'd be inclined to think . . ." She left the proposition dangling. Some things were better left unsaid.

"There's four of us can ride," Joel inserted. "The rest's all got nicks or scrapes bad enough to keep 'em afoot."

"Fine. I'll see to helping the wounded. Then we'll leave to find what stock we can."

"The Rev'ran's been quite good at that, so far, but I reckon he would welcome some help," Joel advised them.

While Rebecca set about caring for the wounded, Lone Wolf made a survey of the wagons. He found two intact, needing only the grim reminders of the Paiute attack removed. Four more, including two heavy freight rigs, could be easily restored.

"We'll need jacks, wrenches and about five men," he declared. "Take the tongue from that burned freighter and put it on this one. Three of you get busy removing undamaged wheels for replacements on these two wagons."

Under Lone Wolf's skilled direction, work moved along quickly. Rebecca found the demands of tending the wounded too much, so she detailed a roundup crew to leave shortly after noon. Under the hot sun, the men continued to labor.

By late afternoon, three wagons had been outfitted. Another day would see the survivors on their way again. Joel Benchley fumed and fussed and cursed a blue streak while he rummaged through the remains of his cooking utensils and set about preparing the evening meal.

"Consarn heathen devils. Misbegotten offspring of a she-goat," he groused. "Damn all them redskin savages to the hottest corner of hell. We'll have jackrabbit stew and what-th'-hell beans for supper," he managed when he paused for a long breath. "Biscuits, too, if that thin pan don't burn 'em."

"Sounds good to me," Lone Wolf offered as he turned from tightening a hub nut. He straightened and pointed to the east. "Look. The men are coming back. It appears like they have ten, twelve head of mules."

" 'Bout time there's some good news around here," Joel snapped. He paused long enough to pare off a thin sliver of cut plug and pop the potent tobacco into his mouth, then bent over the cast-iron kettles on a trestle over a small fire.

Rebecca stood up to watch the welcome arrival of draft animals. For the first time that afternoon, a smile touched her lips. The child she had been tending whimpered and she bent once more to her work.

"There now, it'll be all right, honey. I'm putting that smelly moss in the cut to make it heal better."

"Wh-what's that needle for?" the little girl asked, big-eyed with worry.

"To close the wound. A nip here and a nip there and you'll be good as new."

"Will it hurt?"

"No. Well, only a little. It's just like sewing up one of your dollies."

"We-ell, if . . . you say so." She thrust out her arm.

Deftly Rebecca closed the slash with a bent bone needle and buffalo-gut sutures. She wiped away the last of the blood and bandaged the child's upper arm and shoulder.

"Now, be a big girl and rest quietly while I help someone else."

"Thank you, Mith Rebecca," the small one lisped.

"We saw signs of more," the good news came when the riders entered the battered camp. "It was gettin' on to dark, so we'll have to go after them tomorrow."

"Praise the Lord for that," Ian Claymore intoned. "One large question remains: What can we plan to do for the young women who were taken off?"

"Not much, I'm afraid," Lone Wolf offered.

"I'm not so sure," Rebecca countered. "We have what? Six men able to ride? That's eight of us altogether."

"Don't forget me."

"You, Reverend?" Rebecca asked Ian, surprised.

"I used to be a fair shot back in Kentucky."

"He kilt 'bout five Injuns when they attacked this morning," a pug-nosed, sandy-haired youngster declared.

"Surely not that many, Toby," Ian responded, ruffling the boy's hair.

Toby Andrews crinkled his face, causing his generous collection of freckles to writhe like living things. "Well, you did a bunch, Rev'rend." His candid blue eyes spoke the truth. "Said we oughta kill 'em all an' let

God sort 'em out."

"*Toby!*" his wounded father exploded, scandalized.

"It's the truth," Toby answered, small fists on his hips.

"So it is," Ian Claymore admitted. "Which brings us back to the problem of the abducted women. You said there might be something we can do, Miss Caldwell."

"Make it Rebecca. And, yes, I'm certain we might be able to manage something. A trade for goods, or ammunition. Didn't I see cases of cartridges on that freight wagon?"

"You sure did, Missy," Joel informed her. "Only . . . well, ah, tradin' ammunition to Injuns. That ain't exactly legal, is it?"

"Leaving those girls with the Paiutes is a great deal more immoral than that is illegal, Mr. Benchley," Rebecca countered. "What we need to do is set out a scouting party while we get these wagons under way. After the damage they did, they won't expect for you to be moving again. That should buy us some time. Once we know where the girls are, we can decide how to get them free."

"You've lifted my spirits a good deal, ah, Rebecca. And, I'm Ian to my friends. When should this scouting party be sent out and who's to go?"

"Tomorrow at first light," Rebecca answered. "Anyone not needed to find more livestock and get the wagons on the road can go. Provided they know something about tracking and such."

Claymore frowned. "That don't leave a lot of people. Joel, your friend Lone Wolf, and myself, as I see it."

"Don't leave me out," Rebecca told the minister.

"Why, I . . ." Astonished, the minister ran out of words.

"She's tracked men from the Dakotas to Oregon and through half of Texas," Lone Wolf informed the surprised minister. "Caught most of them, too. Then brought an end to their evil ways."

"How do you mean?"

"I killed them, Ian," Rebecca answered levelly. "Just like you did those Indians this morning."

Chapter 4

An odd assortment set off into a rosy-hued dawn to search for the spot where the Paiutes had joined up after taking their divergent routes away from the ambush. From that point, it would be easy to follow the sign right to their main camp. Behind them, work commenced again on repairing wagons and tending livestock. A few early mourning doves and a determined crow serenaded Rebecca Caldwell, Ian Claymore, Joel Benchley, and Lone Wolf as they separated to scout the different tracks.

At a quarter to ten, the separate trails followed by Rebecca and Ian joined up, heading in a meandering course to the southeast. Each, for similar reasons, found the prospect of the other's company quite pleasant.

"How is it that you're traveling far out here to pursue your ministry?" Rebecca inquired, once they had described their experiences tracking to where they had joined, and had exchanged a few minutes of pleasantries.

"I'm only twenty-five. Back East, that's considered far too young to have one's own parish. We Scots who are Protestant are a conservative lot, I fear. I attended the best Presbyterian seminary in the United States. At least from the view of a man with a name like Claymore. I had another disadvantage in the eyes of the governing board of the Presbytry. Being unmarried is a particular drawback for a minister, you see."

"You *are?*" Rebecca bit at her lip. Damn, she'd made that sound too eager. "Uh . . . I mean, you being single is a handicap to someone committed to giving his time to others?"

Ian favored her with a warm smile. "Not the way I see it." He sighed. "But, then, I'm not on the board. They gave me a choice. Assistant pastor in a small southern town at an even smaller church, or fourth assistant at St. Andrew's in New York. That, or enter the mission service for a few years, with the implied intention that while I'm at it, I should acquire a wife."

"Nice folks you work for." Rebecca's cattiness was not directed at Ian.

"It's . . . what God wants me to do. Or at least I thought that when I left the Kentucky hills to study for the ministry."

"And now you're not so certain?"

"My conviction hasn't wavered. It may be dented a bit, but I'm going to give it a try. I'm to minister to a small, obscure tribe of Christianized Indians. The Cocopa. There are but a few of them. Also some Yaqui.

"From what I hear, the Yaqui are rather savage. About a hundred years ago, some Scots freebooters settled at the northern end of the Sea of Cortez, where the Colorado River debouches into that body of water. For good reason, the Spaniards left them alone and so did the Mexicans later on. That land is shared by the Yaqui and the Cocopa. My fellow Hiburnians managed to convert a few of the natives and even intermarried. Now, they're seeking a regular minister."

"And you're it."

"By choice, I assure you, Rebecca. Not that I'm all that adventurous, but I have some knowledge of living in harsh conditions, of hunting and fishing. In my conceit, I thought I might use those talents to bring a more practical application of religion to the daily lives of my charges."

Impulsively, Rebecca reached across and laid a hand gently on his. "And you will. I'm sure of that." At Ian's brief frown, she hurried on. "I'm not patronizing you. The way you handled yourself during that raid shows you're made of the stuff half-wild natives need to enlighten them to your higher message."

Rebecca made no move to take her hand away, and neither did Ian. He gave a curt nod, as though to confirm to himself the wisdom of her words. Then he scanned the horizon.

"Rider coming down from the north," he remarked in a casual tone.

"Yes. It's Lone Wolf. We must be getting close to the Paiute rendezvous point."

Ian produced a boyish grin that animated the freckles across the bridge of his nose. "I'm learning a lot about tracking from you two. I appreciate that. And I must add, you're the prettiest teacher I've ever had."

Feigned shock formed Rebecca's expression. "Why, such flattery from a man of the cloth of all things."

"I . . . don't mean to be bold. No, that's exactly what I mean. I admit it set me off balance to learn you've killed several men in your time. It's not morbid fascination, believe me, Rebecca. But . . . I, ah, find myself strongly attracted to you."

Rebecca offered a light smile. "You'll get over it."

Utter seriousness colored Ian's words. "What if I don't want to?"

"Then . . . we'll have to deal with the matter when

the right time comes."

"When would the right time be?"

"After we find out about the Paiutes. Tonight, maybe. Back at the wagons."

"Rebecca . . ." Ian hesitated. "I . . . don't want you to get the wrong impression. I mean . . ."

"Nonsense. I don't have the wrong impression at all. We're both healthy, young, grown people. We know . . . what it is we mean. Worrying at it with words, like a dog with a bone too big for itself, can only complicate matters. Let's leave it until then, eh?"

"Looks like we're getting closer," Lone Wolf hailed as he crested a low swell and rode down to where Rebecca and Ian waited.

Rebecca pointed to a distance-purpled clump of saw-toothed hills. "Their main camp probably lies in among those crags."

"That's my guess," Lone Wolf agreed. "All we have to do is locate Joel and we'll know for sure."

Half an hour later, the trio came upon Joel Benchley, who sat on a knobby tuft of loam that protruded from the shelter of a large boulder. He gnawed on a long stem of saw grass and his eyes twinkled when he rose to greet them.

"What took you so long? By the number of sign I read here, them Paiutes musta gone off into those hills. Reckon they've got a war camp there, or a whole village?"

"That's something we can find out tomorrow," Rebecca told him. "For now, it's good enough to give us a way to go."

"If we stay here overnight, there's a good chance we might be spotted," Lone Wolf offered.

Rebecca brightened. "Good a reason as any to head back. Let's hope the volunteer wranglers found more livestock."

Amazingly, due to a little ingenuity, seven wagons had been made trail-worthy, including two of the heavy freighters. Spirits had lifted considerably among the survivors, who rushed to greet the scouting party, babbling gaily about their progress and calling for news of the hostiles.

"We've got them located," Rebecca said quietly. "Or at least we think we do."

"If it ain't their main village, it's a mighty big war camp," Joel Benchley opined. "We figger to get a look at it tomorrow."

"The wagons are ready to move and we have enough stock to do it," Jim Andrews declared.

"Good. Nothing says you can't go right ahead first thing in the morning," Rebecca told him.

"If we know where the heathen bas—er, devils went, and you find out the size of their camp, what do we do about it then?" Jeeter Jenkins, one of the teamsters inquired.

"A good question," Lone Wolf agreed. "Actually, we've got three choices."

"What's those?" Jeeter wanted to know.

"We can leave a scout or two, to keep an eye on their movements and give warning if they come out to raid again," Rebecca explained. "Or we can ignore them entirely and go our own way. Lastly, we can go in and fight them and do what we can to get the girls back."

"Not but one choice the way I see it," Jim Andrews declared in a bass rumble. "We go kick those Injuns' tails and free the captives."

"Rescue is a noble goal, Mr. Andrews," Rebecca returned mildly. "But we have to keep sight of one certain thing: Without a doubt, there are more of them than there are of us. There's little gained from riding in

41

gloriously, to free the captives, only to die in the attempt. No. What we need to do is find a way to be clever. To outsmart the Paiutes as well as outfight them."

"And that will take time," Lone Wolf added. "While we're tending to that, the wagons can be far down the trail, away from the threat."

"If those of us what can fight stay here to do this outsmartin' and all," Jenkins inserted, "who does the driving?"

"Everyone who can," Joel Benchley contributed. "Long as we're on a clear trail south by west, with nothin' but jack rabbits and lizards to worry about, the women can drive the wagons."

"What about me?" Toby Andrews piped up. "I can handle our team easy."

"That's the spirit!" Joel enthused before Toby's father could lodge an objection. "Any boy of twelve or so can handle a six-up, so long's they're not runnin' wild or bein' chased by Injuns."

"Who'll do the scouting for us?" Martha Simmons asked in a timid voice.

"Well, I ain't long on lots of hours in the saddle, or nights on the cold ground. Rheumatiz' got me sort of bad. So, if you folks agree to it, I'll take on the jobs of those we lost."

"You'll do just fine, Joel," Ian Claymore assured the aged scout.

"Yes," three more survivors agreed.

"That's settled then," Ian Claymore concluded. "The wagons will roll at dawn. All able-bodied men will remain here with Brett, Rebecca, and myself. Then we'll go get a look at the Paiutes."

After an evening meal of cornbread, beans, and salt pork, the weary journeyers settled down for the night. By mutual, unspoken agreement, Ian and Rebecca set out for a leisurely stroll outside the perimeter of wagons.

"You haven't told me much about yourself," Ian began once they had gone beyond earshot of camp.

"Yes, I have. Or rather, Lone Wolf did."

"That's all there is to your life? You hunt down men and kill them?"

Rebecca gave a small, nervous laugh. "Not really. I was born on a small homestead in northern Nebraska. We lived there until shortly after my fourteenth birthday."

"Your father was a farmer?"

"No. But that comes later. I had two uncles, Virgil and Ezekiel. They were ne'er-do-wells who easily got in with the wrong sort. A man named Jake Tulley ran a gang of rustles and small-time robbers. They were hiding out at our place that summer. A band of Oglala was raiding in the area. They came to the farm. Tulley and his men thought they were hostile to us and fired on them. That started the fight.

"In the end, to save their own lives, my uncles and Jake Tulley traded my mother and I off to Iron Calf and his braves. They also gave the Sioux some whiskey and ammunition. For the next five years, I lived in the Oglala village of the Red Top band. While there, I learned the truth about my father."

"Uh, pardon me, Rebecca, but I don't quite follow. The truth about what?"

"Iron Calf was my father. Back when the Sioux were actively fighting settlers in Nebraska, a raiding party came to the Caldwell place. Iron Calf was a young warrior at the time. He, ah, took my mother by force. I was the product of that union."

"You must have hated him."

"I didn't know. Mother didn't either, until she recognized Iron Calf. It . . . affected her mind. Anyway, to

43

make this shorter and less painful, I eventually learned to live with my fate, and married a handsome young warrior named Four Horns and bore him a child. Both of them were eventually killed in a Crow raid. I was compelled to take another husband or live in poverty, so I did."

"You were how old at this time?"

"Eighteen."

Astonishment opened Ian's eyes widely. "Why, you're hardly older than that now."

Rebecca stopped abruptly, turned to him, and placed both small hands on Ian's broad chest. "Old enough, Ian. I became a woman before I fully stopped being a girl. In the process I learned a great deal about myself. In particular, that I prefer to be very direct when dealing with a man. If I have reason to dislike one, I waste no time in letting him know it."

Smiling sweetly, Rebecca stepped closer and began to gently rub her palms over Ian's shirt front. "If my feelings are the opposite, I make that clear also. And there's nothing on this earth that will keep me from getting that man in my bed."

Ian Claymore could only stammer. "Rebecca, I . . . well, I mean, I . . . er . . . that is, I, too, feel a strong attraction to you. To some, your life might seem bizarre. It only . . . stimulates me to, well, to have a strong desire for . . ."

Rebecca stood on tiptoes and kissed him on his open, hesitant lips. "Then why do we dawdle away time on meaningless words? Man of the cloth or not, Ian Claymore, you're my kind of man."

He put his arms around her then and drew Rebecca close to him. She felt his warmth and the rising firmness at his groin. She sighed contentedly. In silent invitation, she raised her lips again for his kiss.

Pent-up passion, unfettered by any sense of embarrassment, put ardent urgency into Ian's kiss. Rebecca welcomed it and longed for more. She drove her pelvis against his swelling manhood and ran her fingers down the back of his neck. When they at last broke contact, Rebecca found herself breathless.

"Where can we go?" Ian asked, his voice broken by gasps.

"How about one of the scavenged wagons? No one goes around them," Rebecca suggested.

"We ought to have . . . that is, we need something to protect our clothes."

Rebecca's throaty chuckle sent shivers of excitement up Ian's spine. "Who'll be wearing clothes?"

"I'll get a blanket anyway and meet you at the burnt-out freighter."

"Do it quickly, Ian. Oh, do hurry."

With all the flustered trepidation of a young maiden on her first assignation, Rebecca waited inside the dark shadows of the partially burned freight wagon. The crunch of a footstep set her heart to pounding. Was it Ian? The unidentified night perambulator ambled on by.

Someone coughed. Was it he? Another foot-tread. Light, that of a woodsman. Ian!

"There you are," he breathed in a whisper near her back. Rebecca turned, startled by his soundless approach. He held a blanket over one arm. With the other he reached out to draw her to him. A galaxy of delight exploded within her as their mouths met, tongues explored, heartbeats blended. Ian slipped a hand under Rebecca's pert achingly erect breasts, squeezed gently. In her turn, she slid a hand downward until she could encompass the thick bulge of his straining penis. She stroked. Ian moaned softly and increased the pressure on her left breast, thumb and forefinger teasing the rigid nipple. Their embrace ended on a long sigh.

"What was it you were saying about clothing?" Ian murmured.

"Only that we wouldn't be wearing any." With practiced skill, Rebecca matched her words to her intent.

She slid out of the elk-hide dress and laid it aside. Ian gazed with awe on her light, bronze body, made even more glowingly lovely by soft moonlight. Fumblingly, he began to tug at the buttons of his trousers.

Rebecca reached for his erect member, eager to continue her pleasure. Ian took a step back, spread the blanket, and motioned to it invitingly. The sweetest of smiles on her lips, Rebecca came to him and sank on her knees before him.

She kissed his knees, flicked the pink tip of her tongue along the inner sides of his thighs, and then continued her luscious trail upward.

"You're so delightful, Rebecca. You make me forget all my vows."

"Surely a Presbyterian minister is under no vow of chastity."

"Only outside marriage. But then . . . here you are and so am I. I can no more deny my enflamed desires than I can ignore your loveliness."

Gently he spread her legs, fingers exploring, giving thrill for thrill, while she grasped his manhood firmly and stroked it with an increasing rhythm. Ian bent forward and his lips closed over one sensitive nipple. Rebecca arched her back, used her free hand to draw him nearer, and readied herself for their first magnificent joining.

When his heart came near to bursting, Ian thrust forward at the hips and brought his heated maleness into contact with the wellspring of Rebecca's lusty nature. She shivered, consumed with ecstasy, as Ian slowly, ever so slowly entered through the lacy petals into the heart of her amorous flower.

Deeper, deeper he went, while songs of consummate praise echoed in the halls of her mind. She set her feet firmly on the blanket-covered boards and gave a mighty heave of her pelvis.

"Aaaah!" she cried. And this was only the beginning.

Much to her delight, as the hours drifted by, she discovered over and over that even preachers could be hotly devilish in the privacy of a wagon bed.

Chapter 5

A thick, gray smoke haze hung over the valley. Not a leaf fluttered in the windless night. Cook fires twinkled all through the haphazard village, the traditional bark-and-thatch huts gathered in family groups, lacking the order and symmetry of the plains tribes. A big council fire blazed near the narrow creek that trickled through the basin. Seated in a group to one side were *Kwina-Pagunupa, Tazinupa,* and two of the most influential warrior-society leaders, *Kamododaka* — Rabbit Ears — and *Huna* — Badger. With them, incongruously, considering the recent attack on the wagon train, sat three white men.

Doake Evans, Gage Simmons, and Cord Macklin were long-time friends of the Paiutes. Evans, a man in his late thirties, who had a tendency to run to fat, had supplied whiskey and firearms to the warlike *Kupado-kado* family band for some four years. His small pig eyes glittered with greed at the comforting realization he was now being paid twice for what he did. He had also had past dealings with the *Toedokado*, but the Tule Eaters lacked the fearsome nature of their cousins, the Ground Squirrel Eaters. He sat at ease, stubby legs crossed, a cup of fermented berry juice before him.

"I've got something that tastes a lot better than this," his gravelly baritone voice declared.

"Whis-key," Eagle Cloud mouthed. "It is good. It frees your mind. But not now, Ev-ans. After we've run out the white man, burned his villages, taken his horses, and eaten his cattle. Then we'll drink whis-key with you."

"It's a good time for war, Eagle Cloud," Evans agreed. "To the south of you, the Apaches are stirring up trouble, led by Geronimo and Natchez. The soldiers are few in your country. We've brought you powder and ball, caps for the older rifles. Also cases of ammunition and some new rifles."

Kwina-Pagunupa smiled. He nodded his head and looked around the group. "My medicine is strong. Star has made it so. Yet our men die. The whites' bullets don't miss them as they're supposed to. Why is that?"

Tazinupa's yellowish, cat-eyes centered on his chief. "You're strong, where they are weak, Eagle Cloud. You see the scars that mark my body. They don't come from my enemies, but from the many tests I endured to perfect the Way. I have given you the secret of that Way. Such things aren't for all men's ears. Some hear and know not. Some see and believe not. These will fall aside, even as I told you before."

Eagle Cloud nodded solemnly. It was as he had thought during the fight at the wagons. Men of little faith. Before he could make a reply, Rabbit Ears spoke up.

"Evans, you and Macklin bring us many things to fight with. We raid a ranch, we kill a few whites in their moving villages. We don't need so much ammunition, bullets, powder. What's the reason behind your gifts?"

Eagle Cloud translated and sat back, as curious and expectant as his trusted lieutenant. Macklin and Simmons looked nervous, he noted with pleasure. Evans merely glowered in an attempt to stare down Rabbit Ears.

"It's war, *Kamododaka*. Total war against the whites who have stolen this land. We're on your side. And, sure, once you've won, we'll leave too, so that you can live here in peace. I said before that the Apaches are fighting in Arizona Territory. Now is the time for the Paiute to bring arrow and fire to all who defile your special places. Strike at the mining camps, burn the ranches, destroy the village the whites call Virginia City."

A great radiance bloomed on Eagle Cloud's face. The words Evans spoke were like his own. It couldn't be better. He had his own dream, one in which all the red men rose up like a mighty dust storm and scoured the whole of the far west clean of the ugly pale-skinned ones. With men like Evans it could be done. Naturally, once their use had ended, they would also be removed forever from the sacred land. Eagle Cloud raised his eagle-wing fan to signal he wished to speak.

"You speak good words. Ones we like to hear. But tell me, how are we to raise enough fighting men to attack all the whites?"

"Call on your brothers: the *Kamadokado*, the *Tōedokado*, the *Kuyuidokado*, *Agaidokado*, and the *Sawaktodo*. You are many. Right now, the whites are few. But their numbers grow every day. Think on this and tell me your answer. But, I must know it today. There are other white men who wish you well, who need to know in time to be gone before the fighting begins."

"We'll talk of this. Leave us now, Evans. Go find food. Eat, drink whis-key, rest yourselves. When we have an answer, I'll send for you."

Palest dawn saw the wagons on their way. The

scouting party headed for the saw-toothed ridge where they suspected the Paiute camp to be located. Little Toby Andrews, puffed with pride, brought his team into line with precision that surprised Joel Benchley and his father. As threads of dust rose from the wheels, the riders grew small in the distance.

"We'll split up, come at them from different directions," Rebecca and Lone Wolf had decided.

"Ummm. There's bound to be more than one pass through the low range," Ian Claymore agreed.

"We'll take separate directions where the different trails join," Lone Wolf suggested.

An hour of hard riding after leaving the wagons, they reached the designated spot and each went a separate way. Lone Wolf went straight ahead. His would be the most dangerous route. Ian Claymore took the northern path, burning inwardly with the desire to find his sister and free her. Rebecca swung to the south, headed for the lower peaks that delineated the termination of the the volcanic outcrop.

The rugged, jumbled formation grew larger and more forbidding as time passed. Rebecca constantly scanned the cuts and slashes in the basaltic rock for some sign of a passage. She found little to encourage her.

She turned her spotted-rump horse further south, hopeful of locating an opening, a stream bed or some sort of fissure that would give her access to the interior. They had to return to the wagon train before nightfall. That had been agreed upon. Meanwhile, they had to penetrate the forbidding ramparts and locate the Paiute warriors. Through the morning, Rebecca rode, her search so far fruitless. High noon came.

Darkness where it shouldn't be, in the direct glare of midday sun, excited Rebecca's curiosity. She rode in closer. Yes . . . overhanging walls of volcanic rock shut out the vertical shafts of sunlight. A canyon of sorts. Or at least an arroyo. It offered promise of a way in. Without hesitation, she trotted her Appaloosa horse, which she had named Śila in the Oglala tongue, for he was sometimes given to be mischievous, into the wide, low mouth of the fissure.

Coolness soothed her as she left the desert heat beyond the jumble of upthrust volcanic slabs. Rebecca patted Śila's neck and the Appaloosa snorted in appreciation. Faintly, from far ahead of her, Rebecca could hear the rushing of a waterfall. Only during a cloudburst or the spring thaw would the stream reach out to the parched sand, she knew. She would go on, Rebecca decided, and maybe find what they sought.

Half an hour at a walk brought her to the waterfall, without finding any sign of the Paiutes. She dismounted and gave Śila a long drink. Then she knelt and refreshed herself from the chill, pure stream. A basin had formed at the foot of the falls. It beckoned invitingly. She had a job to do, Rebecca chided herself, no time for swimming now. The narrow gorge bent around the jutting ledge that created the small cascade.

When she inspected it, she found the way too narrow for Śila. Greenery grew in profusion. She hobbled her mount and set off on foot. Gradually, as it had been doing for some time, the natural pathway gained in altitude. Disappointingly, it also narrowed to near impassability. At last, her progress became reduced to pulling herself up by handholds made of protruding rocks. All possibility that this constituted one of the ways to reach the Paiute camp had vanished. Yet, she wanted to go onward, learn where, exactly, this wedge in the hills led. Doggedly, she continued.

Nearly halfway to the top now, Rebecca reached out and placed her hand on top of another rough boulder. Perspiration trickled down her high forehead into her large, startlingly blue eyes. She blinked at the salty sting and pulled her weight upward. Her head had barely cleared the large rock when she heard the dreaded sound.

A whirring rustle, like the dry voice of death came from above.

With a hiss like escaping steam, a huge rattlesnake reared up and prepared to strike. Rebecca froze a moment, shocked at the sight of the fat coils, the huge triangular head, gleaming fangs. A good twelve-button set of rattles again sounded ominously. What could she do?

She couldn't risk a shot that might alert the Paiutes. Couldn't, for that matter, reach her sixgun in time. The big, menacing head weaved for a moment, tongue flicking to sense the exact location of the target. Slowly, Rebecca reached with her left hand for the slender skinning knife she carried at her waist.

With pain searing her right shoulder as it bore her entire weight, she drew the weapon and inched her arm upward. Point at an angle, she made ready to take a slash at the deadly snake.

Then the rattler struck.

Swift as a darting trout, Rebecca swung. Instinct caused her to jerk her head back from proximity to the boulder, and her right hand let go. In the moment before she fell, Rebecca felt a sharp scrape on the middle two fingers of her hand. Then she dropped.

Air blasted from her lungs when she hit the floor of the arroyo. Numbed, aching, she lay there, wondering about the pain in her hand while darkness surged up and engulfed her in unconsciousness.

Chapter 6

With all the stealth his years as a Crow warrior had taught him, Lone Wolf eased himself into position among the trunks of two stunted cottonwoods, growing in a jumble of gray-black, igneous boulders. Outcasts of an ancient volcanic eruption, the huge stones had lain in a cluster for centuries. From this vantage point, he could see down into the spreading valley.

Gray smoke plumes rose from cooking fires dotted among the bark and thatch lodges. Close to where he crouched, half a dozen Paiutes stood near the council fire. With them, Lone Wolf was surprised to discover, were three white men. He had managed to maneuver himself in close enough to hear their voices, without being detected. Unfortunately, he could not understand the Paiute language.

"*Kwina-Pagunupa* is ready to give you his decision now," *Tanzinupa* told the three glowering whites.

"About time," Cord Macklin growled when another Paiute brave translated.

"My friend's right. Eagle Cloud said before yesterday was over. It's near onto sundown an' he's only now gonna see us. *We're* the ones with the guns. You need 'em. So what's all this about?"

54

"Evans, you lack the calm a man of wisdom should have," Eagle Cloud said chidingly in English as he stepped from his low bark lodge.

"Shit! Two damn days we've been here. We've gotta get back to, ah . . . awh, never mind."

Lone Wolf listened with interest as this exchange took place. Guns for the Paiutes. They had strength enough to nearly wipe out the wagon train. What would they be needing more weapons for? He listened with care while the man Eagle Cloud called Evans went on complaining.

How long had she been unconscious? With the severe overhang of the arroyo walls, she could not use the sun to gauge the passage of time. A perpetual twilight filled the narrow gorge. The snake!

With a stab of worry, Rebecca Caldwell recalled the rattler which had struck at her before she fell. She looked around, brow creased with concern. Over to the left she saw movement. The headless body of the huge reptile. It still writhed in its death throes. A good sign she hadn't been out for long. Then she raised her right hand, her body icy with trepidation.

It wasn't swollen. Relief oozed through her tense figure. Two fangs had ripped long gouges in the soft leather of her glove. Rebecca quickly removed it. Thin red streaks showed on the back of her middle fingers, but the skin had not been punctured. She had struck fast enough with her skinning knife to render the viper's attack ineffectual. The aches in the rest of her body suddenly became intensely obvious.

"Oh!" she said aloud. Then, "Damn."

She'd lost her precarious purchase on the ledge and fallen a good fifteen feet. Her back ached and she was aware of raw spots and scratches. Her bottom felt as though she had spent a day breaking wild horses in the manner of white ranchers. Whatever the case, wherever the Paiutes had their camp, she had definitely not found the way in. With a muffled groan, Rebecca raised herself to her feet.

Head bent downward, one hand on her sore buttocks, she began to search for her knife. She located it in a clutter of loose rocks at the foot of the slope from which she had been dislodged. She sheathed it and hobbled over to where Šila munched unconcernedly at clumps of grass.

Rebecca released the rawhide string that kept him from straying and put it in a saddle bag. Then she raised one moccasin-clad foot to swing into the saddle. "Steady boy," she urged as the Appaloosa shied sideways at the smell of snake and snake blood.

Astride her mount after great effort, Rebecca pointed his nose southward and started out of the treacherous canyon. "If I tell Lone Wolf and the others about what really happened," she speculated aloud, "I'll never hear the end of it."

Bustle best described Virginia City, Nevada, seat of Storey County in the west-central part of the territory. Wagons, which consisted of barely more than tongue, wagon tree, and running gear, raced along the wide main street. The drivers hurried to the pine-bristling hillsides to pick up their loads of newly-felled and cleaned ponderosas, to speed back to town and dump at building sites or the sawmill, like their previous cargoes. Dust, wood and coal smoke filled the air of the cup-like valley.

Anvils rang in half a dozen forges, blacksmiths busy making nails and truss straps for the flurry of building going on. Their apprentices, when they could hire any, sweated to throw more coal on the glowing burners. The great rush was to rebuild the town, which had been devastated by fire in 1875. The Comstock Lode still poured forth silver and gold in such attractive quantities that the population had grown to over thirty thousand souls. Before the conflagration, the populous city had boasted six churches and a hundred saloons — a proportion that some wags considered to be just right. Disincorporated as a city following the disaster, Virginia City had been reincorporated only this year, which accounted for the spurt of growth.

To the more fastidious residents, the Fourth-Ward School represented the superlative in architectural splendor. The large, Victorian-style building, with a full brick basement and three stories done in clapboard and ornate rococo ornamentation towered over many lesser structures.

To Roger Styles, the Crystal Saloon exemplified his own preference. It sported huge, glittering cut-glass chandeliers, inch-thick carpets, and liveried waiters. These latter slid noiselessly over the rich floor covering, serving bonded bourbon and imported brandy in goblets of rock crystal. The food in this establishment had been described by one visitor as 'sinfully Babylonian and sybaritic.' For an extortionate sum, Roger had retained a suite of rooms upstairs to serve as living quarters and office.

More often, though, he held court at a secluded table in one corner of the main salon, isolated from its neighbors by ornate, wicker-work screens. The white linen on the round oak table, the silver service always laid out in anticipation of a sumptuous repast, and the ubiquitous rock crystal goblets went well with Roger's surroundings and his style of living.

Roger Styles was a promoter. A hustler. A charlatan, a thief, and a murderer. He was also a survivor.

57

Unlike the more uncouth practitioners of his chosen profession, who frequently decorated the gallows or telegraph poles in Virginia City, Roger Styles had class. On this particular late afternoon, Roger sat at his table—like a fat spider at the center of his web—absorbed in the pages of the city's major newspaper, the *Territorial Enterprise*. He paused to chuckle over an outlandishly humorous news story written by a young journalist, Samuel Clemens, who had signed his by-line as Mark Twain. Roger lifted his goblet of brandy and sipped from it.

Over the rim, he observed a prosperously dressed gentleman approaching his table. Wendell Porforey, owner of one of the banks Roger used to cleanse his illicit fortune, smiled broadly under a thick walrus mustache. He swept his hat from a round, bald head and extended a pudgy hand for Roger to shake.

"Aha! I thought I'd find you here at this time, Roger. All this activity gives a man a mighty thirst. I'll have the usual, Charles," Porforey diverted to instruct the waiter who had glided up. Then he took his seat.

"Is it true what I've been hearing, Roger?"

"What's that, Wendell?"

"That you're actually looking into buying a lot of the burned-out properties? In many instances, the owners have moved on, left no trace of where they've gone. The titles to the land may be clouded. It's a risky venture, I'd say."

"Buying rebuilt places would cost more, and there's no guarantee the property value would increase."

"That's an astute observation, Roger. Only, what do you base it on?"

"The Comstock isn't going to last forever. Eventually all mines play out. When the silver runs dry, the town will, too. Before then, I want to buy cheap and sell dear."

Porforey chuckled and patted his ample belly, which protruded beyond the waistband of his trousers. "You seem to have done well enough at that in the past, considering the size of the deposit you made in my bank."

Roger, his graying blond hair now dyed jet-black and parted down the middle, all natural curliness removed by a thick application of pomade, leaned back in his highly polished captain's chair. His icy gray eyes studied the fat fool across from him and he chuckled inwardly.

If Porforey only knew the source of that sizeable sum, or the reason why Roger felt so certain about making a killing in Virginia City real estate, the lard-bellied banker would pop a blood vessel and die of a stroke. Yes, he'd carefully thought it out on his solitary ride here from Pendleton, Oregon. Roger had fistfuls of money — his own and others', taken from the bank in Pendleton before he made good his escape from that detestable bitch, Rebecca Caldwell. For several long days he had speculated on what he could do with it. Then the idea had come to him.

Riches abounded in sparsely settled Nevada Territory. Only one community, Virginia City, had a large population. If a panic could be created . . . say, by an Indian uprising, many of those less-than-stout-hearted would sell out and run for safety elsewhere. It was an old scheme, actually. One he had employed before in one form or another. That the previous attempts had met with failure could be laid at the feet of Rebecca Caldwell. Curse that woman! With effort, Roger returned his concentration to the banker.

"I've heard the Paiutes have been raiding again," Roger remarked off-handedly.

Wendell frowned. "Strange you should mention that in connection with our present conversation. But, yes, they have. They're an intractable lot. Hate all white men and most other Indian tribes. Army would have rooted them out to the last papoose if the war hadn't come up. By 'Sixty-one, their chiefs were well ready to talk peace and to accept life on a reservation. Then the troops went East to fight the Johnny Rebs. Since then the war talkers among the Paiutes have gotten them stirred up all over again."

"Not to mention that another generation of warriors has come of age to fight," Roger added. "Considering my intention to speculate in real estate, what would a large-scale Indian scare do to my investments?"

Porforey worked his fat lips in and out as though savoring a tasty dessert. "If you bought at the present prices, it could be ruinous. If you bought when everyone wanted to flee, you could later realize an enormous profit, when the army settled accounts with the hostiles."

"As would my banker and, ah, partner?" Roger gave Wendell a conspiratorial wink.

"A-hem. I had not, er, considered such a possibility. However, as your banker, I must advise you that your investing might be more to your advantage if the savages do engage in a general uprising."

"Thank you, Wendell. I always value your advice. Now, let's order, shall we? A dozen or so oysters on the halfshell to start. Some good sherry with them, eh? Then, after we've had time to appreciate them, we'll look into what the chef has for tonight's dining fare."

Perfect, Roger rejoiced in his mind. He had read Porforey exactly right. Not what one could call totally dishonest, but not adverse to capitalizing on the misfortunes of others. So long as the banker never knew that Doake Evans, Gage Simmons, and Cord Macklin had been employed by Roger to insure a territory-wide uprising by the Paiutes, the greedy old lard tub would be content to get richer and never worry about the means. Eagle Cloud was a firebrand. Evans and his men could ignite him easily.

Then—oh, then!—the money would pile up in Por-forey's bank faster than it could be counted. He would own an entire territory all for himself, Roger gloated.

Chapter 7

Long shadows slanted eastward when Rebecca caught up to Ian Claymore on the way to the rendezvous point. Try as she might, she could not entirely conceal her discomfort as they rode through the day's waning hours. Ian asked about it and she found she could not keep her vow of silence.

When she finished, rather than laughter, a sigh of relief came from the young minister. "It must have been a miracle that saved you. First that rattlesnake, then the terrible fall. It's a wonder you didn't break any bones."

"Or be bitten by the snake," Rebecca added gratefully. "I'm certain that the Paiutes are somewhere in that low range. You found nothing and neither did I. From the marks here, Lone Wolf hasn't come ahead of us. Maybe he'll have better luck."

"Just, ah, how, er, sore are you, Rebecca?"

The longing, hungry look in Ian's eyes told her the source of his question. "Not so it would interfere with . . . something important. There's a willow grove around that water hole. What say we detour, rest our horses, and, ah . . ."

"Make love in the sunset?" Ian asked eagerly.

Rebecca's happy, willing smile answered him amply.

They tied off their reins to willow branches. A blanket roll from Ian's saddle skirt made a perfect trysting spot. Rebecca hummed happily as she removed her clothing. Ian studied her raptly.

"Those bruises and scrapes—they'll take a while to heal," he said, concerned.

"They won't interfere, dear Ian. Get out of those clothes and lay on your back. That way my battered back won't be aggravated."

Grinning, Ian complied. He had a magnificent shape, Rebecca thought as he removed his coat, shirt, and trousers. Impulsively, the naked nymph stepped forward and slid her hands along his sides and over his pale white buttocks.

"Ummmm. You feel good to me. We really shouldn't take the time," Rebecca suggested half seriously.

"Oh, but we will, my love. We definitely will." Ian lay down as Rebecca had suggested.

A wistful smile playing about her lips, the lusty young woman sank to her knees, then reached out and encircled Ian's pulsing phallus. Gently she stroked it.

"Ian, you make me feel so good. I'm certainly no stranger to love, but there's . . . something about you that fires my blood."

"Stop talking and make love, woman. The sunset'll be over if you don't."

"We'll make our own bursts of color," Rebecca promised.

Wild delight spread through her veins as Ian entered her body. Slowly, Rebecca began to sway in a circle, easing bit by bit more of him into the core of her being. It was magnificent! At last she had received all of him. A shudder of ecstasy rippled up her spine and she forgot all about her injuries.

Sunset colors lingered in the west and blended with

hues of pure elation that rose as Rebecca worked toward her first, of what she knew would be many, pleasure-filled peaks.

Supper became a sort of somber celebration at the place where the wagons had stopped for the night. Lone Wolf had returned with his report on the Paiutes. He had counted forty-six lodges. Too many for a war party. Too many, even, for a family band, Joel Benchley declared. This was a gathering of the people. And one, obviously, for war.

"I make it to be sixty, seventy warriors already," Lone Wolf stated. "From the sign, more are coming every day. Worse, there were three white men there. Not captives. They had wagons loaded with weapons, ammunition, whiskey, and medical supplies. Looked like outfitters for the army." He paused, frowning.

"From what I could hear in English, the Paiutes are planning a big uprising. The various bands are sending men. The leader is called Eagle Cloud. He claims to have medicine that makes himself and his men invulnerable to bullets."

"Horse droppings!" Joel Benchley exclaimed.

"Of course," Lone Wolf agreed. "So far as the warriors go, that's obvious. I did see Eagle Cloud wearing a padded breastplate of some sort. It's stiff. Makes his shoulder movements restricted. He has to turn from the hips. My guess is there's some sort of iron plate inside the cloth cover."

Ian Claymore's eyes brightened. "That accounts for why I hit him dead center with a load of double-oh buckshot and didn't even scratch the bugger."

"Hummmm." Lone Wolf considered that a moment. "So, we can say that Eagle Cloud's medicine is definitely manmade. Some sort of armor. There are many

stories of war chiefs and warriors called ▒▒▒▒
The first was a Comanche who found an old
cuirass. Others, among the Kiowa, the Pawnee,
the Kansa, made similar discoveries or had copie▒
made. For the most part, these pieces of armor can
turn any arrow or lance, stop a musket ball, or bullets
from most small-bore cased ammunition."

"I'm willing to bet they won't turn a forty-five-
seventy round," Ian stated confidently.

"You're right about that," Lone Wolf agreed. "Only
right now we're a bit short on Springfields."

"No we're not," Jeeter Jenkins, the teamster injected.
"There's a case of civilian models in that wagon of
mine. I can break 'em out if you want. Lots of
cartridges, too."

"Then do it."

Rebecca Caldwell had remained thoughtfully quiet
during the conversation, speculating on the alterna
tives they had. The wagons could continue on south,
eventually travel out of the area contested by Eagle
Cloud. Or they could make a dash for Virginia City,
warn people of what might be in store and see that the
word got spread. Or they could do something to
prevent the impending war.

"If we're going to stop Eagle Cloud, now's the time to
do it," Rebecca said quietly, her mind made up. "Before
he gets too many reinforcements."

A circle of astonished faces surrounded her.

"I mean it," she said forcefully, pounding one small
fist into the palm of her other hand for emphasis. "We
can leave early in the morning. Lone Wolf can lead us
there. We'll need to make a thorough detailed study of
the Paiute camp, then lay careful plans. There's something, somehow, we can come up with to break Eagle
Cloud's power."

"Yeah, but what?" an uncertain Jim Andrews in-

it out once we know exactly what
. I say it's our only chance to be
and to prevent widespread killings of
ut Nevada Territory."

ne Wolf declared strongly.

"A...   el Benchley added.

"It's my sister who's out there, so I'm going," Ian Claymore announced.

"All right, dang it," Rafe Baxter relented. "Let's all go. You womenfolk who can shoot and drive wagons can stay with the youngsters."

"Th-thank you all," Rebecca told them in a soft voice. Tears of gratitude and relief brimmed in her eyes but didn't spill over.

All of the signs could be clearly read—the obvious prevalence of many unshod hoofprints, the absence of game, not a sight of another human being, and an all-pervading silence in the wide cut into the purple mountains. Even the birds kept out of sight, and only an infrequent jay scolded or a high-flying hawk screeched its hunting call. The Paiutes, and a lot of them at that, had used this passage frequently. The scouting party, directed by Lone Wolf made slow, cautious progress.

"They may have lookouts posted," Ian Claymore suggested.

"Most tribes never do. That's how the Oglala camps got surprised so often by Crow and Pawnee raiders," Rebecca answered. "How the Dakota easily ambushed their enemies' villages, too," she finished with a flicker of a smile.

Her body still tingled from lovemaking and her eyes glowed when she turned them on the young minister.

Ian grinned foolishly and seemed lost in some distant, remarkably pleasant memory.

"The Apaches are supposed to use sentries," Lone Wolf added. "They and the Paiutes have been allied in the past. No telling what we might run into. I didn't spot any yesterday, though."

Half an hour dragged by in the twisting, turning passage. The small group saw no enemy signals given. Not even natural animal cries interrupted the silence now. Like the throb of a giant heart, though, a distant beat began to pervade their consciousness.

"War drums," Rebecca said in a hushed voice after several minutes.

"Unh," Lone Wolf agreed. He'd seen those responsible for the martial sound the day before and didn't feel any too anxious to encounter them again.

"Five miles, would you say?" Ian asked.

"More like eight to ten," Rebecca answered. "There's a lot of drums playing."

Midday came and the four whites didn't pause to prepare a meal. Rebecca and Lone Wolf passed around strips of elk jerky, obtained from the Nez Percé, and handfuls of dried berries. They all munched in silence and washed their meager meal down with fresh, cold water from a narrow stream. Not a cloud dotted the sky. The only thunder came from the throbbing war drums of the Paiutes.

When the crash and roar hurtled toward them from the canyon, Rebecca and her companions were caught totally unprepared. A flash flood. Wherever the rain had fallen, it had been far enough away to give no warning.

A wall of brown, muddy water, white-foam-capped, rushed toward the startled people. Pushed ahead of it came a treacherous abatis of small boulders and up-rooted trees. Cacti whipped and whirled in the roiling

67

torrent, along with the bodies of small animals trapped in the deluge.

"Flood!" Lone Wolf shouted, jerking hard on his reins and kicking his mount's ribs to speed it upslope, away from the watery menace.

Quickly the others did the same, hurrying to escape certain destruction. They divided according to their positions, Rebecca and Ian to the right, Rafe Baxter following Lone Wolf to the left. Within seconds, murky liquid swirled around their horses' hoofs and the rattle and clack of tumbling limbs, trunks, and sage brush sounded loud in their ears. Sure-footed, the Appaloosas ridden by Rebecca and Lone Wolf surged ahead. Ian Claymore's mount whinnied shrilly, showing the whites of its eyes, and its hind quarters slipped in the uncertain footing.

Yanked backward, the young minister's feet came free of the stirrups. Within another split second, he would fall into the tumult. Unbidden, a cry of alarm ripped from his throat. Rebecca turned and plunged downslope.

Clawlike, Ian's hand groped outward. Rebecca's fingers closed around his wrist in the same moment his horse regained its footing. Upright in the saddle again, Ian gasped his thanks and they both strained upward to evade the racing course below.

Onward it boiled, while the four struggling humans urged their panicked animals higher. "Are you all right?" Rebecca yelled.

Her words lost in the calamitous boom of the swift juggernaut, Ian could only watch her lips move. All the same, he nodded agreement and pointed up the gorge, where bits of the land, altered now by hydraulic scouring, had begun to appear above the crest.

Only seconds had passed, yet the deadly cascade receded with the same speed it had first come upon them. The rumble of its passage lingered, while returning silence confused their ears.

"It's over with," Rebecca breathed with relief.

"We're lucky to be alive," Ian asserted.

" 'Lucky'? That's a strange word for a minister to use," Rebecca teased.

Ian smiled ruefully. "Sometimes, even He needs a little help from Lady Luck. Let's go over with the others."

"The ground will be slippery. Might even be some sinkholes. We'd better ride along above the high-water mark and join up later."

A freak of nature, the destructive flood had originated in a side canyon. At its junction with the route to the Paiute camp, the four riders regrouped and continued on. A mile further, Lone Wolf signaled for a halt. Everyone dismounted and hobbled their horses. Then began a long walk.

On foot, Rebecca and her companions covered another mile and a half, then crawled on hands and knees to the top of a ridge. The sight revealed below filled them with awe and an icy touch of dread.

Chapter 8

"They are so many," Rebecca barely breathed.

New bark lodges had been added since Lone Wolf had observed the growing village the previous day. Tom-toms throbbed, dictating the very pulse of their own hearts. All about the helter-skelter of dwellings, warriors swaggered, brandishing weapons ranging from war clubs to modern rifles. Only a few women were visible.

"There are more every day," Lone Wolf said regretfully.

"I wonder where my sister and the other girls are being kept?"

"We won't be able to find that out in daylight, unless they're let out to do labor for the warriors. After dark, though . . ." Lone Wolf suggested.

"Ian," Rebecca injected, "I want to get them back every bit as much as you. Right now, though, isn't the time to take risks. If anything alerted the Paiutes to our presence, it could be disastrous. Not only for us, but for everyone with the wagons. We had better stick to what we came for, and work on that when we have a better chance of success."

Ian sighed heavily. "You're right, of course."

From an inner pocket of his coat, Ian took a leather-bound notebook, which he used for jotting down ideas for sermons. In the careful, meticulous hand of an engineer, he began to record the location of every lodge. While he worked, Rebecca and Lone Wolf identified the significance of each.

"There, at the center. That's Eagle Cloud's lodge. It's the largest," Lone Wolf declared.

"The one across the big fire ring will be the shaman's dwelling. It's also sort of a shrine in most cases," Rebecca added. "Those nearest to the ones we've shown you will be guards for Eagle Cloud, war leaders, and chiefs from other bands. See the way the women keep away. Look. There's the shaman now."

Tazinupa stepped from the low entranceway to his lodge and stretched himself to full height. The jet, raven-feather shawl he wore draped over his shoulders and upper arms added to his stature. He had the sun-bleached skull of a fox woven into a high spill of hair, the glossy black tuft bound by a copper ring. He raised his arms and spread them wide, then began to speak in a high, singsong voice.

"Warriors of the Paiute. Ground Squirrel Eaters, Trout Eaters, men of the Tule Eaters, *Kuyuidokado* and *Sawaktodo*. This day I make you mightier than all the whites. You'll never fear their bullets again. You'll have the same magic that protects *Kwina-Pagunupa* from the guns of the whites. For two days you have danced and sung the songs. You purified your spirits in the waters of the sacred stream and in the sweat lodge. Now you are able to receive the secrets that will make you powerful beyond all other men."

"They've got warriors from every band of the Paiute,"

Lone Wolf whispered to the others.

A mighty, full-throated roar rose as the warriors cheered Star's announcement. Many rushed forward. While they did, Ian continued to make his drawings. Suddenly, he drew his breath in sharply.

"Hester. That's Hester down there."

Ian pointed to a slender young woman, her head and shoulders bowed under the heavy burden of a load of bound limbs for the fire. Sunlight made reddish glints in her dark brown hair and her fair complexion decidedly marked her as a white person. She stumbled through the camp as though in a stupor. Anger flooded Ian's face and his scowl could have halted an enraged bull. He saw not only her fatigue and servitude, but her torn dress, blood stains on the ripped left sleeve, the dejected droop of her shoulders, her bare and bloody feet.

"Damn them," he hissed.

"At least she's still alive," Rebecca reminded him. "Look carefully. Maybe you can identify the others."

Long minutes passed without success. He saw none of the other captives. When Ian signified that he had completed recording the entire layout, with what names and ranks had been provided by the others, the scouting party quietly withdrew. Back at the horses, they breathed easily for the first time in three hours. Wordlessly they tightened cinch straps, freed their mounts, and took to the saddles.

The ride back to the meeting place with the wagons seemed endless. Now that they all realized the danger presented by the Paiute fighting force, they anxiously wanted to relate their findings to the others and lay specific plans. They smelled woodsmoke and cooking odors long before sighting the circled caravan.

After a filling meal, Rebecca and Ian called a council of war.

"There are a lot more Paiutes in those mountains than we expected," Ian began. "I saw my sister. She's being used as a slave. Somehow we have to figure a way to get in to free her and the others."

"What about my Lucy?" Mrs. Freeman inquired.

Ian shook his head sadly. "I saw none of the other captives, Liddy. All we can assume, hope for, is that with Hester alive, they must be also. Here's a plan of the camp I drew. Pass it around and study what you see. Then maybe we can come up with some ideas."

"Looks to me like it'd take the cavalry and some artillery to blast those savages out of there," Jim Andrews offered as he passed on the pencil sketches.

"Too many for us to fight, that's for sure," Jeeter Jenkins lamented.

"Not necessarily," Rebecca countered.

While the discussion went on, Ian had been making new sketches in his notebook. Brow puckered in concentration, he would make a line or draw a circle, shake his head, then erase some portion. Eventually, he nodded in satisfaction and began to draw rapidly. When he completed his work, he rose to get attention.

"I've been listening to what you've all said while I worked. Everyone knows there are a lot of Paiutes up in those mountains. They're making up for war. Too many to take on at once. But what say we do it piecemeal?"

"Fine, only what's to say they don't send out enough of those red devils to ride right over us?" Jenkins asked.

"We've no guarantee of that. But we can do something about it if they do. I've been working on this little idea. I know it should work the way I have it set up.

73

Now, as I understand it, these heathens are superstitious."

"Of course," Joel Benchley snapped. "Any fool knows that. Uh . . . pardon Rev'ran'."

Ian smiled. "The point I'm trying to make is that they can be easily impressed by things they know nothing of. I've had some small experience with blasting powder and Mr. Nobel's new dynamite. There's plenty of both in that freight wagon."

"True enough, Reverend Claymore," Jethro Barnes admitted. "Only, surely, the Paiutes know about dynamite and artillery."

"Yes. They've fought the army for more years than some of us have been alive," Lone Wolf agreed.

"Give me a moment, if you please. Look at these sketches I've made. I think you'll agree the Paiutes have never experienced dynamite in this particular form."

"Dang right," the boss teamster admitted. "I ain't never seen the like either."

"I'm sure you haven't, Jeeter," Ian answered calmly. "Because I've just invented it."

What he referred to was a drawing of a large square box, with a second, round cylinder inside. Circles had been drawn between the two containers. The gathered men and women stared at the device in confusion. Ian grinned boyishly and explained.

"The inner cylinder, it could be a peach can or any such, is filled with dynamite and tamped down. Between it and the outer one, a large tinned beef can or something like it, are stacked columns of pistol balls. Jeeter, you said that a number of bags of small-caliber balls were among the trade items in the freight wagon, right?"

"Sure is, Rev'rand."

"Good, then. We have a ready supply of the two most

74

vital ingredients. If we have fuses and detonator caps in quantity, we're all set."

"We got that, too," Jenkins assured him.

"So we can make a big bang and throw a few pistol balls around. What good does that do us?" Silas Miller, a constant complainer, injected.

"Since dynamite explodes in a spherical pattern . . . in other words, in all directions equally, unless it's confined in a pocket of rock or tamped under a stump, it should spray a whole lot of those balls out at anything in the way." Ian paused and grinned again. "Like Paiute warriors, for instance."

"Ian, that's a marvelous idea!" Rebecca enthused. "Only if they go every which way, how can we be kept from being hurt? How do you make sure the balls go where you want them to go?"

"We set up posts around the circled wagons, say a hundred feet out. On the back sides we wire a heavy rock. On the other, my little, uh, Claymore bomb, pardon the conceit, is attached. The fuses are lit at such a time so that the first line of attackers is past the posts before the bombs go off.

"If the posts are set in such a manner, with plenty of backing material, so that the spray overlaps, any Paiutes beside or in front of them will be showered with balls and bits of shredded metal. The result would be disaster for the enemy."

"They'll think it's magic," Joel declared.

"Which gives me another idea. Lone Wolf," Rebecca began to her friend. "Are you practiced enough in some of the Crow power road medicine to give a good showing in front of the Paiutes?"

"Enough, I suppose," he allowed modestly.

For several years before he had encountered Rebecca in the Oglala village and aided in her escape, Lone

Wolf had been a practitioner of a special sort of medicine. Known to various tribes by different names, the spiritual seeking of the power road made severe demands on those who would pursue it. One of them was celibacy. Lone Wolf had attained an extraordinarily high degree of proficiency for one not born into acceptance of such forms of religion. Now, for the first time, he was being called upon to demonstrate his powers. For a long moment, doubt assailed him. Reason dictated, though, that if his attainments could help in the present situation he could not, in clear conscience, refuse to do what he could.

"Can you make smoke appear?"

"That's an easy one."

"What about flying through the air?"

Lone Wolf shook his head and studied the ground. "I've heard of it being done. With some luck, and a little diversion, I suppose I could manage it somewhat."

"What about restoring life to something that is dead?"

"That takes time and a lot of energy," Lone Wolf said candidly. "I've seen it done, and even assisted once with a warrior who had been mortally wounded. Not just one good shot, but several wounds that could kill. My medicine teacher and I worked on him for three days. He rose up on the fourth, asked for water, and rode back to the village. Later, he lived long enough to sire three sons before he died. And even then, he was killed in battle, as he had been meant to be all along."

"Unbelievable," Ian gasped. "Not that I question your truthfulness. Christ and his disciples healed the sick and raised the dead."

Lone Wolf grinned shyly. "It's sort of the same thing, I think, Reverend Claymore. The way I see it, the pathway is identical. It's only the words that are different. All I can say is that I'll try."

"Well then," Rebecca decided. "It's time to go make peace with the Paiutes and free the captives."

"How?" a chorus of voices rose in question.

"That," Rebecca answered enigmatically, "will be a matter of a little of Ian's special violence and Lone Wolf's magical talents."

Chapter 9

Only a few of Virginia City's most dedicated, full-time drunks lined the gleaming mahogany in the Crystal Saloon so early in the morning. Upstairs, in his comfortable suite, Roger Styles glared across the short distance that separated him from Doake Evans.

"That red nigger's getting too big for his loincloth," Roger growled. "We're providing him weapons and all he needs. Where does he come off telling you to wait until he's ready to decide whether to take them or not."

"Eagle Cloud's got this big medicine now, Mr. Styles. Supposed to make him an' his warriors bullet-proof. Least he thinks it works. Don't think he needs anything from whites anymore. But he *is* talkin' war. That's what you wanted, right?"

"Yes, Evans, that's what I wanted," Roger returned tiredly. "I don't care what sort of lunatic belief he holds. I only want to make sure he's well enough armed to keep the uprising going long enough to start panic-selling of homesteads and city lots. You and your men are in for your share. You don't have to worry about making a profit off of providing guns and ammunition to the Paiutes. Whatever Eagle Cloud offers in trade, take it. If he makes you wait for his pleasure . . . well, then, I suppose that's the way it'll have to be. We don't need to like it, but we do have to live with it. When and where is he going to make his next attack?"

"There's some ranches along the lower west slopes of the Humboldt Range. Eagle Cloud and his warriors are going to start raiding them three or four days from now."

"That, at least, is good news. Now," Roger went on, rising, "let's go downstairs. I'm in the mood for breakfast. Some bacon, eggs scrambled with herbs and onions, and champagne. How's that sound?"

"I call that livin' mighty high on the hog."

"Get used to it, Evans. You're going to be in a position to appreciate the finer things in life right soon now."

Night creatures made their usual noises, strident or in hushed susurrations, as Rebecca Caldwell and Ian Claymore made their way through the mountain pass. A sharp chill, which penetrated their clothing, became a harbinger of the rapidly approaching fall. The pair had chosen to return a night later, in an attempt to locate the captives, while Lone Wolf and two men followed behind a party of Paiute warriors which had left the large camp before sundown. Each, with practiced skill, moved silently through the thick growths of pine, alder, and lupin. An owl's sudden hoot froze them in place.

"Did that sound real to you?" Ian inquired in a whisper close to Rebecca's ear.

Rebecca replied with a light touch on Ian's right forearm and a nod of agreement. "It isn't likely the Paiutes would have put lookouts around after so long a time. We'd better hurry. The whole camp should be asleep before we get there, but we need all the time we can use."

When they reached the edge of the huge Paiute encampment, Rebecca again silently cursed the casual disorder of the village. With a plains tribe, their task would have been easy. All they would have needed to do is start at the center, keeping quiet to avoid discovery, and work their way around each successive hoop until the captive women could be located.

"We're going to have to split up," Rebecca told her companion. "I'll head to the right, you go the other way."

"We meet back here in an hour and a half, is that all right?"

"Yes. It should give us time enough."

Soft snores and mutters came from the thatch-and-bark lodges as Rebecca moved quietly through the family-band gathering. She listened closely for any sound that might betray the presence of a white person. Half an hour passed without results. Then she heard a whimper from one low, crude dwelling. Silent in moccasin-clad feet, she slipped in closer.

"Oh, no. Please no. Not again," a tormented voice quietly appealed in English. "Ah! Aaaah! It hurts so."

She'd found one of the captives. Only which one? Rebecca sincerely hoped it wasn't Hester Claymore. The grunting sounds from inside made it obvious what the prisoner cried out against. Rebecca made a note of which lodge and moved on. A check of the star positions told her the time neared when she was to rendezvous with Ian. She had to hurry now.

From another bark dwelling, some twelve paces away, she heard subdued sobbing. Rebecca eased her way to the side closest and listened for a long moment, doubtful of finding another captive so easily. At last a faint whisper came through the wall.

"Oh, God, deliver me from this evil." The speaker had a distinct Kentucky accent. Could this be Hester Claymore?

Rebecca placed her lips close to the thatch and barely breathed out the words she spoke. "Quiet. Say nothing. Help is on the way, so take heart."

"Oh!" a startled gasp followed.

"Shussh," Rebecca cautioned. "Are you Hester Claymore? Only the smallest sound, mind."

"Y-yes," came a sibilant whisper.

"We'll be back for you. Be brave," Rebecca advised. Then she crawled away from the lodge to prevent further conversation.

The remainder of Rebecca's inspection proved fruitless. She started back to the large pine, which had split a huge reddish boulder, where she would contact Ian. A few steps less than a hundred paces from the spot, a slight, dark figure rose before her in the night.

Instinctively, Rebecca lashed out with a small, hard fist. She struck the youthful Paiute in the throat. The force of her blow prevented him from making any cry of alarm. Only a muffled gagging sound came from his lips. Quickly, she hit him again. This time with the barrel of a Smith and Wesson .44 American revolver.

His knees went slack and he tumbled to the ground. Rebecca tucked the big six-gun back in the beaded belt at her waist and bent to grasp him by the shoulders. When she rejoined Ian, she panted slightly from the effort of dragging the unconscious brave to a secure place.

"What have we here?" Ian inquired with mild amusement.

"He's hardly more than a boy," Rebecca whispered. "Probably had to go out and relieve himself. Too bad for him. I'll tell you more when we get him further away from here."

"Did you find any of the girls?"

"Yes, two. Did you?"

"Only one."

"The second girl I located was Hester," Rebecca told him happily.

"You're sure?"

"Absolutely. Now, give me a hand with this one, will you?"

Together, they hefted the body and carried the senseless Paiute back into the rocks to a place beyond hearing from the village. By then, the youth had begun to come around. Roughly, they dropped their burden.

"*Ni kiwani*," Rebecca said in Lakota, then repeated, "You are awakening. Do you understand me?"

"*L-Lakota sansunta*," the youth muttered.

"I gather he doesn't speak whatever that was," Ian observed.

"Sioux," Rebecca told him, then bent back over the prisoner. "Do you speak English?" she asked slowly.

"Little. Speak trade, talk wis-key man."

"What does Eagle Cloud plan to do?"

"*Kwina-Pagunupa* kill all whites. Make go away like storm in summer."

"How do you mean that?" Rebecca demanded.

"N-no words."

"Does he mean he won't talk?" Ian asked.

"More likely he can't explain it. Trade English is a long way from being fluent. When will *Kwina-Pagunupa* start to kill the whites?"

"Now. Warriors go one sun past. More when sun come next time. Soon all whites die."

Rebecca continued her attempt at interrogation with scant success. At last she stood upright, her back aching from remaining so long in a stooped position. She arched herself and, even in the dim moonlight, the graceful, feline movement sent a moment of thrill through Ian Claymore.

"There's nothing more we can get out of him," the white squaw said with finality.

"You'll turn him loose then?"

"And have all those Paiute warriors on our backs before we can get out of this canyon? No. I don't like it. He's helpless, after all. But we're going to have to kill him."

Shocked, Ian stared a long moment. "I can't quite adjust to the idea of such a cold-blooded act," he protested. "Can't we tie him up and leave him for the others?"

"How long before anyone knows he's missing? A search would have to be organized. By then, they probably wouldn't find him in time and that would be a far more cruel death than a knife in the heart."

Ian swallowed. "You're hard, Rebecca. A lot harder than I expected. Yet, won't the results be the same? When they find the body they'll know someone's been around."

"Granted. Only, by the time they back-trail us, we'll have had opportunity to set up a nasty demonstration to convince them to forget about their little war."

With a sigh of regret, Rebecca drew her knife, bent down and drove its sharp blade into the frightened, wide-eyed Paiute's heart. When she withdrew it, a gush of warm crimson flooded over her hand and forearm. For a moment she felt her stomach churn and lurch.

Then she remembered Bobby O'Tolle and what he liked to do to little girls—and what she had done to him.

"I'm sorry, Ian. It was necessary. We'd better get away from here fast."

Most wounds had healed enough so that the men

83

and women of the wagon train could participate in setting the stage for the expected Paiute attack. In pairs, the heartier men sweated under the hot sun of the next day. With post auger, shovel, and tamping bar, they set into a place a ring of low oak post. Each had to be positioned according to Ian's careful calculations.

"No, turn it a bit. That's it. Straight up and down, now. Easy," he would call out as each pillar of hardwood went into place.

"Tamp it well. You fellows over there, bring a good-sized rock, will you?"

What Ian meant turned out usually to be flat-faced boulders of basalt or other igneous rock that taxed the strength of the pair hauling it. These, they wired to the backsides of the posts. Other, flatter, rocks were wired to the fronts, pointing outward, away from the circled wagons. Most of the day went by in this arduous labor. Content at last, Ian called a halt.

The sweating, staggering men made straight away for the water barrels. Ian headed for where trestle-type tables had been set up on saw horses. There, Jeeter Jenkins supervised a group of seven women, Silas Miller, and Toby Andrews.

"How's it coming, Jeeter?" the reverend inquired.

"Fine as frog fur, Rev'rand."

A bright and skillful man to hold his position as a head teamster, Jeeter had been the natural choice to direct the construction of the deadly devices Ian had so cleverly designed. He had set two women to opening thick-walled beef tins and dumping the contents into large cast-iron kettles. Another pair opened an assortment of round containers; apple and peach cans, those for dry biscuits and other commodities. The empty containers they wiped dry and passed along to Silas Miller, a tinsmith by trade. Considered a complainer by nature and reputation, he nevertheless plied his tools with deft ability.

"Those look good, Silas," Ian commented to him. "The cylinders are centered perfectly."

"Peach cans make the best," Miller replied in a tone that implied he had somehow been questioned on his ability. "Puttin' the ribs in for the stacks of balls is easy."

"How many do you have completed?"

"Better than a dozen, but it ain't enough."

"True. We'll need more. At least twice that many more."

"Ain't enough hours in the day," Miller objected.

"We must do our best then. Miss Rebecca and her friend Lone Wolf are scouting the backtrail we left. They'll give plenty warning before the Paiutes get here."

"They better," Miller growled.

At the next station in the assembly procedure, the remaining women and Toby Andrews meticulously stacked rows of pistol balls into the spaces between the metal vanes. Tamping and preparing the power charges were tasks Ian had reserved for himself to do. Considering that, he realized he had better get at it.

An open case of dynamite sat at the far end of the collection of crude tables. Ian seated himself and began to slit open the waxy paper that covered the explosive sticks. The contents he poured into the cylinder of the rough bomb before him. When he had it half full, he took a wooden rod and tamped the grainy substance firmly, packing it to a third of its former volume, then began to open more sticks and fill the casing further.

"Hester is still alive," he muttered under his breath. "She's not lost her spirit and she knows we're coming to help her."

He'd finished the first device. From a small box on the table, he took a blasting cap and grabbed up a coil of fuse. Carefully he hefted the deadly device and carried it to one of the prepared posts. Two men held it in place while Ian wired it into position. Now came the hard part.

Ian had already cut several foot-long sections of fuse and timed their burning rate. He knew fairly well what to expect. Unfortunately, his dangerous inventions had to be put much closer to the wagons than he had hoped. From his hip pocket, he removed a brass crimping tool. He took the loose end of the fuse coil and inserted it in the open end of the cap. Then he crimped it tightly into place. This he inserted in the face of the compacted dynamite and covered it all with a wad of putty. Lastly, he gave attention to the large roll of fuse.

Slowly, he unwound the black cord. The men would bury it later. When he reached the right spot, he cut the length free and returned to prepare another charge.

"Gonna be an interestin' night, 'pears like," Joel Benchley observed as he stopped to watch the young minister at work.

"I've no doubt of that, Joel," Ian responded. "Are the rifles being taken care of?"

"Jeeter's got two men on passin' those Springfields out to the best shots. Them Paiutes can have all the iron shirts they want an' it won't do 'em no good now. When you figger we'll be ready?"

"Some time tomorrow afternoon."

"Yep. Sure hope them idgit Paiutes don't take it in mind to attack before then."

"Amen to that, Joel."

Unfortunately, a small contingent of Paiute warriors, fired by the enchanting rhetoric of Eagle Cloud and Star, had no idea of the important of more time for the vulnerable wagon-train people. Confident in their invulnerability to bullets, they attacked the wagons within five minutes of spotting them.

"Indians!" a man setting in a post shouted. He ran for the protection of the circle.

"They're coming back!" Silas Miller exclaimed. "I told ya so."

"Don't look like there's many of 'em," Joel remarked calmly. "You fellers with the Springfields, give 'em till they get in to about two hundred yards, then knock a few outta their saddles. Let's see how they like that."

Chapter 10

Five warriors formed a staggered vee at the head of the attack. Ten men, armed with Springfield rifles, took careful aim on the center of the Paiutes' chests and held steady. Over the notched sights, the figures grew larger.

"That's it. Hold on. Hold . . ." Joel commanded. "*Now!* Fire!"

Two short of a dozen, the heavy 500-grain infantry slugs sped toward the charging targets. A miasma of smoke masked the space in front of the rifle muzzles. Like fall's last leaves in a gale, the quintet of braves were whisked from their mounts' backs to tumble in the grainy desert soil. Instantly, those Paiutes behind their hapless brothers reined to the sides and whirled away.

"Reload. This time we wait until they get in closer, then everyone open up."

Ian Claymore was tempted to light the fuses on the three of his special bombs nearest to the raiding party. He withheld, though, confident as Joel was that this was only a probe. The big show would come later. Instead, he readied his big Purdy shotgun and waited.

Only moments passed before the Paiutes launched another dash in the direction of the circled wagons.

Wiser now, they had spread out. The space of several riders separated each warrior. Hoofs pounded the desert soil, as they drew nearer . . . nearer. Still the whites had not shot at them as before. Their leader could see the strained, sweating faces of the men and women who held guns aimed at their direction.

"Fire! Give 'em hell!"

Puffs appeared along the line of defenders, like gray-edged clouds that spat thin lances of fire. The medicine? What about the magic of *Tazinupa*?

Those questions flashed through the mind of the leader, along with intense pain, as a load of double-oh buckshot smashed through his eagle-bone breastplate and mangled flesh behind it. The lead balls drove splinters of rib bone ahead of them, which slashed lung tissue into bloody pulp. The hot pellets spread more pain, until the brain could no longer handle the thousands of panic messages being sent. In defense of itself, the brain turned off. The leader fell dead along with six more of his followers.

"That did it! They ain't comin' back!" Joel crowed as the remaining Paiutes turned the horses' rumps toward the wagons and sped off across the desert.

For the moment, peace had returned.

"After running those warriors off so easily yesterday, how can you be sure the other Paiutes will be back?" Ian Claymore asked Rebecca Caldwell the next morning.

"We found plenty of signs that the entire camp is on the move. Every warrior is out. You heard Lone Wolf describe the sacked ranches, the people killed to the north of us. When the survivors of your little fracas get the word around, you can bet the whole gathering will be headed our way."

"Only ten more of my bombs to put in place, thank goodness," Ian said by way of reply. "When, do you think?"

"A lot of distance has to be covered. I make it about sunup tomorrow. Little chance the Paiutes can get here before that."

"That's time enough," Ian sighed in relief.

Work went well, though Silas Miller continued to grumble. Before the triangle sent its shivery message through the desert air to summon the workers to the evening meal, all of Ian's radical new bombs had been put in place. Supper consisted of more stew, fruit, and rice pudding, made from the contents of the opened tins. For a change, though, the meal came with fresh, flaky biscuits done up by Joel Benchley. He had plenty of hot, *Ariosa* brand Arbuckle's coffee to wash it down with. For all the assurances of the explosive devices, the powerful, long-range rifles, and their improved strength and health, everyone peered anxiously out into the darkness.

Two people remained unaffected by this mood. Rebecca and Ian exchanged glances, then quietly slipped away from those holding vigil around the big fire. Rebecca's heart pounded with expectation. Memory supplied again the thrilling sensation of Ian's powerful thrusts and his masterful ability to prolong the ultimate completion of their sensual couplings. Tonight would be no exception, she felt sure.

They met in the shadows beyond the circle of wagons. No words were needed as they quickly removed their clothing. A low depression shielded them from observation. Eagerly, Rebecca knelt before Ian and wrapped small fingers around his hardened organ. She stroked it rapidly for a moment, then leaned forward to caress him with her mouth.

Rebecca felt Ian shudder as she teased him with her

90

tongue.

"Aaaaah," Ian sighed softly and grasped the back of her head. He began to thrust with his hips.

Delight filled Rebecca as she sought to draw even more ecstatic responses from her wonderful lover. She ached to have him fill her, yet remained helpless to end her happy ministrations. On she worked, slower now, drawing out the pleasure they shared. Gentleness, born of great love, filled them with glowing warmth.

With rapt attention on his goal, Ian lowered himself between her wide-spread legs and drove his pounding manhood deep within her.

Dawn made the transition from white, through pale pink and orange, to a solid band of pastel blue. Before daylight, the waiting defenders had eaten a hearty breakfast and warmed themselves with tin cups of strong coffee. For many, each progressing minute lowered their tension, made them less confident of an attack. Not so for the experienced ones.

"They'll come," Rebecca said with finality.

"It would have taken a while to gather up all their bands," Joel added.

"This Eagle Cloud is no fool," Lone Wolf contributed. "Once he saw our defenses, he would lay some plan before attacking."

An hour into morning, thin threads of dust could be seen from several directions, coming closer. The slight knoll on which the wagon defenses had been established soon became surrounded by a solid ring of Paiute warriors, three files deep.

"They got here, all right," Joel observed calmly. "You fellers with the Springfields get ready. When they charge, start pickin' off a few at maximum range. That'll give 'em something to think about. We held off

91

a mite the last time. This'll make 'em smart."

Ian Claymore, busy removing the covers that protected the exposed fuse ends, rose. He lifted his arms and spoke in a clear, commanding voice.

"I know this may sound unusual to some of you, yet there's ample precedent for it. Let us all join together in prayer. *Almighty God, who sustained Joshua against the Canaanites at Jericho, who led David to victory over the Philistines, and caused Solomon to prevail over all the enemies of Israel, protect us this day. Steady our hands, sharpen our eyes, and make every shot count. Amen.*"

"That was some prayin', Rev'ran'," Joel declared, eyes bright with admiration.

"Eerie, wavering cries rose from the braves below. Painted for war, gaudy with feathers, their mounts small and wiry, they charged up the knoll, giving a mighty shout. Ian stood in a position where he could be seen by the men at the fuses.

"Remember," he called out. "Light your fuse so that the first rank can get past before the charges go off."

On came the Paiutes, howling in fury. At three hundred yards, the first Springfields opened up. Four warriors flipped off their ponies. Half a dozen more of the .45-70 rifles blasted into the morning. Two more Paiutes went down and four horses died. The momentum of the charge faltered. A steady crackle ringed the defenses, as all the Springfields discharged.

Seven horses and thirteen warriors died in the scything spread of lead.

"Light your fuses!" Ian commanded in a bellow.

Fine, gray grains of powder sputtered and sparkled as black-tinged white smoke rose from the lengths of fuse. The first rank of warriors had nearly reached the upright posts containing the bombshells. Behind these, smaller branches, sharpened at both ends, had been driven into the ground at steep angles. The suggestion had come from Jeeter Jenkins.

"We used 'em once, when we was freightin' inta Oregon Territory. Blackfeet jumped us an' these pickets scared the livin' tar outta them savages. Heard about how they'd been used by peasants against knights back in the old days."

The first Paiutes thundered past the posts.

"Cover your cars!" Ian shouted.

Despite both the cotton provided by several ladies' quilts that was stuffed into their ears and the hands tightly clasped over the outside, the monumental blast that followed brutalized the hearing of everyone on the knoll. A gigantic shock wave traveled through the ground and air, knocking everyone standing to the hard desert soil. Unheard in the cacophony, shrieks of pain came from horses and men of the first rank who had become impaled on the sharpened stakes.

Those who had not, immediately lost their footing and crashed to earth. Rebecca Caldwell watched this infernal spectacle with a sense of disbelief. Nothing could be so horrible, so utterly destructive, as this diabolical invention. Bits of metal and pistol balls shrieked and moaned through the air, slashing into the flesh of the Paiutes and their ponies caught on the front side of the bombs. Those not slain outright received terrible wounds.

Blood gushed from severed limbs, cuts, and gouges in chests. Deafened by the enormous explosion, those men and animals that had regained footing wandered about in total disorientation. Dazed by the power of the blast, many in deep shock from wounds or horror, they acted without conscious direction.

Many stumbled into the waiting muzzles of the defenders. Rifles and shotguns began to detonate, tiny, firecracker pops after the immensity of Ian's dynamite eruption. Some few, less benumbed by the awful ordeal, sought useable horses and began to flee.

Among them, Rebecca recognized Eagle Cloud and his medicine man, Star.

"By all that's Holy, we done wiped them out!" Silas Miller ran to where Ian made an effort to stand. The grouchy tinsmith grabbed the minister's hand and began to pump it vigorously. "I owe you an apology, Reverend. I thought all that stuff of yours was foolishness. But it done worked a marvel."

"Now's the time to send a messenger to Eagle Cloud to explain how all this magic happened," Rebecca remarked. She had removed the cotton from her ears, but her head still rang inside.

"Ummm. Yes. Who should we send?"

"Eagle Cloud speaks English well enough. Anyone could go."

"How about me, Rebecca?" Ian inquired anxiously.

"No. Hester might see you and blurt out something that would spoil our plan."

"What about me?" Joel offered. "I can even speak a few words of Paiute."

"Perfect. Now, here's what you're to tell them," Rebecca began.

Subdued sounds of mourning could be heard in the Paiute village when Joel Benchley, Jethro Barnes, and Silas Miller rode in, clearly displaying the blue-edge belt of white beads that signified a peace mission. Scowling, Eagle Cloud met them before his lodge.

"Many men died. Paiute men. Why do you come asking for peace?"

"We didn't want to be attacked in the first place. Your young men raided us once, burnt some wagons, took off some girls as prisoners. All we wished to do was go in peace. You attacked again." Now came the important part, Joel thought, concentrating on his next words.

"Before this happened, strangers came to help us. A woman of the Dakota and a powerful medicine man of the Absaroka."

"A Sioux and a Crow together?" *Kwina-Pagunupa* asked in disbelief.

"She is seeking men who did her people evil. He is a follower of the Power Road. They do not live as man and woman. Differences are forgotten. Each has a reason. It is his medicine that defeated you yesterday. He and the woman *Sinaskawin* would come and explain it to you. In return they ask for peace and for the release of the captive girls."

A deep scowl creased Eagle Cloud's brow. "I will think on these things. It must be discussed in council. Go now. You'll be told what we decide."

Stories, told by refugees, ran wild through Virginia City. The horrors grew with each retelling. Their number and variety brought a smile to Roger Styles's lips. Soon, now, he could start making it known that he was in the market for land. He only hoped that Evans and his men had managed to make it to Eagle Cloud's war camp with the wagonload of new rifles and ammunition. Then the whole territory would go up in flames. Yes. How nice that would be for him. A bustle at the entrance to the Crystal Palace drew his attention.

Beaming, though trying hard not to show it, Wendell Porforey, the banker, bustled toward Roger's table. "Have you heard?" he exclaimed from halfway across the room.

Roger winced. "Come on over and sit down. Do you have to advertise our business to the whole of Virginia City?"

The chubby-jowled bald man pulled a face of contrition. "I'm sorry. It's only, well, everything seems to be going your way. These Paiute raids are just what you need. Savages are always unpredictable, but their fractiousness has played right into your hands this time. I hope you appreciate the good fortune that has come your way."

"Oh, I do, Wendell, I certainly do," Roger told him drolly.

Chapter 11

Two days had gone by in anxious uncertainty before a delegation arrived from the Paiute village. A party of five was selected to go for the demonstration of power. This included, naturally enough, Lone Wolf and Rebecca Caldwell, along with Ian Claymore, Jeeter Jenkins, and Jim Andrews. When they reached their destination, a hush fell over the whole encampment.

"Don't seem they rolled out the red carpet for us," Jeeter observed in a whispered aside.

"I'm still wondering what to do to impress them," Lone Wolf worried aloud.

"You don't think they're already impressed?" Jim Andrews asked him.

"Lone Wolf's right," Rebecca informed them. "We could have our status of guests changed to that of victims in an instant. The disaster they experienced can quickly be forgotten if we don't back it up with more magic."

"I'm ready as I can be," Lone Wolf offered.

"What about you, Ian? Did you bring along everything you need?"

"Right at hand, Rebecca. Give me some time to wander a bit, and we'll have a show that'll bug their eyes."

A grunt came from their escort and they halted in front of a large lodge. From prior scouting visits, they recognized it as that of Eagle Cloud. After a long moment, while the horses snorted, stamped, and swished at flies, a voice sounded from within. Then Eagle Cloud, dressed in his finest regalia, came from the bark dwelling.

"You are the Absaroka medicine chief?" he addressed Long Wolf in English, his voice heavy with disbelief and sarcasm.

"I am."

"I find before me a white man, yellow hair, pale eyes. This is no Absaroka shaman."

"I am known as Lone Wolf, war leader and follower of the Power Road. I am of the Beaver Lodge band of the Crow Nation, adopted years before this and fierce in battle or medicine. I can see by the paleness around your eyes you have heard of me. Does this satisfy you?"

Eagle Cloud nodded slightly. "What is it you've come to show me? *Tazinupa*, my shaman, has said your people have little power compared to his."

Lone Wolf smiled condescendingly. He snapped his fingers and flames immediately began to play about his right hand. Eagle Cloud stepped back quickly, an "Oh" of surprise escaping him.

"That is only a child's trick. One used to amuse Absaroka infants. If you wish to see what can be done with fire, build a pit, like so . . ." Quickly, Lone Wolf's hands and arms described a long, narrow shape, some five feet deep.

"Fill that with wood and burn it. Then keep on until the pit is entirely filled with coals. Then you'll see the mystery of the Absaroka Power Road."

In his own language, Eagle Cloud ordered it, though his tone sounded reluctant. "Leave your ponies with our herd boys; come, smoke a pipe with me and take refreshments. And show me more of these, ah, child's tricks."

Sleight of hand wasn't exactly what Lone Wolf had in mind. He entered the lodge, his mind fixed on his inner self, directing power to the center of his being, calling on powers and spirits. Slowly his heart rate diminished, his breathing nearly ceased. When invited to be seated, the others did so immediately. Then Lone Wolf sat.

Another gasp from Eagle Cloud.

Lone Wolf, legs crossed, arms across his chest, leaned back in the usual resting position, his body suspended some ten inches above the folded deer-hide robe on which he was to have reclined. Mutters ran among the closest followers of Eagle Cloud and his bodyguard.

"*That*," Rebecca explained sweetly, "is not another child's trick."

"He-he-he's in the air," Eagle Cloud managed to stammer out.

"More precisely, he is not in this lodge."

"How do you mean, woman of the Dakota?"

A moment later, a dreadful yowl came from the direction of *Tazinupa*'s bark dwelling. The shaman had refused to attend this meeting, claiming it to be a cheap imitation of real power. Now another shriek came from his lodge. An apprentice appeared through the entrance, like a cork popped from a shaken bottle of beer. His eyes bugged and his face had turned ashen.

Disoriented by terror, he ran in purposeless circles.

"*Paiudokado!*" he wailed over and over. "*Paiudokado!* He is inside the shrine. He tried to eat my heart!"

Excited people gathered, the camp population much smaller now, after the devastation of Eagle Cloud's war party. The youth continued to shriek and race about for several seconds, then fell over and lay still upon the ground.

"He has fainted," a woman said.

"No," an old man answered sadly. "He is dead. *Paiudokado* ate his heart."

Inside the large lodge of Eagle Cloud, Lone Wolf slowly settled onto the robe prepared for him. He drew a deep breath and opened his eyes. He smiled and turned friendly gray eyes toward Eagle Cloud.

"Well, what is it we're going to discuss? What would you like to see me do?"

"T-the boy who studied under *Tazinupa*? Is he . . . ? Did you . . . ? What magic have we seen here?"

"The boy is alive. Only his fears drove his senses from him. Excuse me, I have been out of my body for a moment. While wandering in the Big Darkness, I met a fearsome creature named *Paiudokado*. Do you know of him?"

"The People Eater," Eagle Cloud explained in English. "T-then you sent him to the shrine inside Star's lodge?"

Lone Wolf shrugged. "A small matter. I suggested to him that there might be some among the Paiutes who didn't believe in him. That perhaps he'd ought to go and visit among them and see who had little faith. Apparently the boy had a great deal of faith."

"I would see no more now. Let's eat and smoke while the fire is being prepared. What is it for, Lone Wolf?"

A shy, fleeting bit of a smile raised the corners of

Lone Wolf's mouth. "That you shall all see later on."

After the ritual meal and smoke for guests, Rebecca and her companions were allowed to walk about the central core of the camp. Lone Wolf performed a few simple conjuring bits which allowed Ian Claymore to slip out of observation of the guards discreetly placed upon them.

With the filled saddlebags over one shoulder, Ian set efficiently about preparing his part of the plan designed to impress Eagle Cloud into releasing the captives and leaving the wagon train to progress in peace. While Ian worked, Lone Wolf held his audience enthralled. Rebecca kept her eyes searching for any sign of the white girls. When the call came that the fire pit had been made ready, she had still seen nothing of them.

While Rebecca searched, Ian completed his tasks. Everything was in place. The long cords had been brought to a central place where he could see the clearing where the long trough of coals glowed hellishly. Already the curious Paiutes had begun to gather. He sought some sign from Rebecca that the captive girls had been located. Disappointment filled him when he saw her give a negative shake of her head. Lone Wolf, accompanied by Eagle Cloud, Star, and several principal men of the Paiute village, appeared at the far end of the shimmering pit.

Lone Wolf stood calmly, with a proudly erect bearing, his face serene, lips raised slightly as though in a trance. Slowly he bent and removed his moccasions.

"What're you going to do?" Eagle Cloud asked, still unnerved by the earlier demonstration.

"I will walk across these coals. Then back to you."

"Trickery," *Tazinupa* snarled.

"Would you care to join me?" Lone Wolf invited.

Silence answered him.

With studied precision, Lone Wolf stepped out onto the shimmering bed. Tiny flames flickered around his feet. Without haste, he made steady progress over the trench. His body glistened with a thin sheen of moisture and the fringed edges of his loincloth began to smolder. Still he showed no sign of pain. At last, only three feet remained. He made them easily.

Lone Wolf stepped onto firm ground and raised first one foot, then the other. Although reddened a bit, no burns could be seen, no blisters. Awed murmurs rose from the onlookers. The place where he stood had been superheated to the point no one could come closer to inspect him. With a wave of his arm, he turned back, closed his eyes in deep concentration of his inner powers, and started back.

Several cried of "No! You'll be killed!" rose from the audience.

Lone Wolf continued on.

Consumed with envy and rage, the shaman, Star, balled his fists and muttered spells and incantations. They seemed to have no effect, as Lone Wolf continued toward where the medicine man and Eagle Cloud stood. When he reached them, he strode placidly out of the inferno, dusted off his feet, and allowed those close by to make a detailed examination.

"Not a blister," Eagle Cloud declared.

"He isn't burnt at all," another war leader gasped.

"This is not magic," *Tazinupa* complained. "Some sort of clever trick was used."

"Shall I call down thunder and lightning to prove to you my power?" Lone Wolf demanded.

Star studied the cloudless sky and smirked. "Yes. You do that."

"What about . . . over there?" Lone Wolf offered,

pointing.

A bright flash and loud roar followed some distance beyond the camp. The ground trembled and a tall pine shuddered, swayed slightly, then crashed to the forest floor.

"And over there," Lone Wolf pronounced, his extended finger indicating another spot nearly ninety degrees from the first.

Once more came the bright light and thunderous noise. Another tree fell loudly to the hillside. Moans and gasps rose among the gathered Paiutes.

"Or there," Lone Wolf challenged.

Ian Claymore pulled the last cord, which ran to an instantaneous fuse igniter. With less than a half-inch of fuse in the detonator cap, the explosion seemed simultaneous with Lone Wolf's gesture.

Down came a final tree.

"What is it you wish of the Paiute people?" Eagle Cloud asked in a subdued, resigned voice.

Lone Wolf breathed easily for the first time. The dynamite blasts had been the only real trickery he had used. His powers had drained him so that he barely had strength to answer.

"Peace with the Paiutes, for us and for the whites who live in the territory called Nevada. Also, the return of the captive girls from the wagon train."

Eagle Cloud's head bowed, chin lowered to his chest. "It shall be as you ask."

"No!" Star shouted. "No. You are the powerful one. Are you not immune to the white man's bullets? Don't do this!"

"Bring the girls," Eagle Cloud commanded, ignoring his shaman.

A stir began in the crowd that formed an open lane, through which some older warriors led the hostages.

Bedraggled and battered, all of them limping, they yet remained alive and bright hope glowed in their eyes. Ian had slipped from his place of concealment and now ran forward, arms wide to embrace his sister.

"Hester," he cried. "Oh, my darling sister."

They clung together for a long while. Hester sobbed softly, her face buried against her brother's strong shoulder. The other young women, though dazed, wandered to where Jim Andrews stood. *Tazinupa* was nowhere to be seen.

"You may all go in peace. The word of *Kwina-Pagunupa* is your guarantee. There will not be war with the whites. That's my final decree."

"That ain't what you agreed to before," a grating voice came from the direction of the shaman's lodge.

Doake Evans, Gage Simmons, and Cord Macklin stood there with Star. Their hands rested on the butts of well-used revolvers. *Tazinupa* raised his arms.

"Warriors of the Paiutes. These whites are few. We are many. Follow the magic of Eagle Cloud. Kill them all!"

Disgruntled warriors, who had not approved of their leader's acquiescence, whooped and dashed off to snatch up weapons. Doake Evans, grinning evilly, drew the Remington at his side.

Before Evans could fire, Jim Andrews swung up his Winchester saddle carbine and blasted off a round that grazed *Tazinupa*'s side, slamming him back into the bark lodge. Pellets, fired at an oblique angle by Ian Claymore, smashed into Evans's gun hand and caused him to drop his weapon. Shouts of alarm came from everywhere. Rebecca drew one of her .44 Smith and Wesson Americans and thumbed back the hammer. A Paiute brave raced toward Jim Andrews's exposed back. Rebecca took quick aim.

A heavy 215-grain slug from the .44 smashed into the warrior's chest, staggering him backward, eyes wide in wonder as life fled his body. Gage Simmons ran toward Rebecca Caldwell, his '72 Model Colt extended to full arm's length. Before he could fire, a close-range slug from Jeeter Jenkins's .45-70 Springfield smacked into Simmons's right ear and exploded out the whole left side of his head.

Gage went face-first into the ground. Meanwhile, Cord Macklin and Doake Evans had consolidated their position and fired at the small force opposing them. Albeit inaccurate, the whizzing bullets caused Rebecca and Jim Andrews to duck and move to better positions. Little cries of alarm came from the former captive girls as they scurried after the stalwart Andrews. Ian lighted a short fuse on a stick of dynamite and hurled it through the entrance to the shaman's lodge.

Tazinupa burst from inside only a second before the blast. The large bark dwelling went up in a shower of splinters. The shock wave knocked the shaman sprawling on the ground. Lone Wolf appeared from where he had been fighting off two Paiute braves. He grabbed up Star by his shaman's robe and hurled him, shrieking, into the fire pit.

Writhing like a condemned soul in hell, *Tazinupa* performed a weird dance of death, howling out his agony. Then he fell silent and slowly slipped below the surface of the glowing heap, limbs and torso already charred a deep black. Ian threw another stick of dynamite, which brought Evans and Macklin out into the open. Rebecca spun toward the former and fired the last round in her .44 Smith.

A miss.

She quickly changed for her other big revolver and eared back the hammer.

Evans turned toward her, a satanic grin twisting his face into a mask of vileness. He had started to raise his six-gun when a large black hole appeared in his forehead and he snapped over backward. Rebecca allowed herself a small smile of satisfaction. Her aim had been perfect. Then white-hot pain seared along her left side, reminding her that the battle was far from over.

"Get 'em, kill 'em all!" Cord Macklin bellowed over the tumult.

"No! Stop. Stop the fighting!" Eagle Cloud roared in his own language.

Some of the braves obeyed instantly. Others, rallying around Macklin, continued to offer resistance. Rebecca felt the hot trickle of blood down her ribs and she favored her left side as she maneuvered to get a shot at Macklin. Jim Andrews was down, she noticed, nursing a bullet wound in his right calf. She shifted further around, keeping a bark hut between her and the combatant Paiutes. Macklin came into view.

A long roar sounded nearby and Rebecca jerked her head in that direction. Ian Claymore stood with his Purdy shotgun at his shoulder. Across from him, in the direction the twin muzzles pointed, Rebecca saw the headless figure of Cord Macklin jitter and sway, twin geysers of blood spewing from the severed stump of his neck.

"Lay down your weapons!" Eagle Cloud commanded once again. "T've given my word. No man who has taken up my war pipe may break it."

A final whoop of defiance came from a warrior who tried to hurl his lance at Ian Claymore.

Lone Wolf and Eagle cloud shot the defiant brave simultaneously. Silence filled the village.

"Go now. You'll have no more trouble from the

Paiutes," Eagle Cloud promised.

Cheerful birdsong greeted the dawn on the next morning as the wagon train started out southward again. Now, only the harsh conditions of the desert remained to torment them.

That would be quite enough, Rebecca Caldwell thought. Yet, a dark premonition nagged at her, saying it wouldn't be all.

Chapter 12

Dust devils danced on the shimmering horizon, while the oppressive heat of the desert beat down on the slow-moving caravan. Rebecca Caldwell's left side itched irritatingly, salty trickles of perspiration running down into the raw flesh of her slight wound. She winced, and Lone Wolf spotted it instantly.

"We're a good four days beyond the Paiute country," he observed. "A day or two of rest wouldn't be out of order, would it?"

"Are you pampering me, Lone Wolf?"

"No. I was thinking of the others. Jim Andrews took a bad hit in his leg. Jeeter got grazed too, just like you. There's little water and the animals are tiring. A rest could do a lot of good."

Rebecca smiled. "You're right. I'd been thinking of it, but something keeps gnawing at me that we ought to make as much distance as we can."

Sila's nostrils twitched and his ears pricked up. Rebecca patted his neck. "Good boy. You've smelled out water. Maybe it's a sign. If there's enough for a stay, we might make camp for a while."

Lone Wolf smiled. "They'll all be grateful if we do."

"I'm doin' pretty good, ain't I, Dad?" Toby Andrews asked his father, voice ringing with pride as he handled the six-up of mules that drew the Andrews' wagon.

"Yes you are, son. Not many a twelve-year-old who could say the same."

"Awh, there was kids who did it on farms," Toby depreciated. "Remember back in Ohio?"

"That's different, Toby. They drove hay wagons in fenced fields, doing farm work. We're covering ground we've never seen before and neither has our team." Jim Andrews patted his son on the leg. "You're becoming a first-class driver."

"Does your leg hurt much, Dad?"

"Some. It itches, which means it's healing. Miss Rebecca got it cleaned out right good and put some powdered stuff in the hole. So far, no redness. What's this?" he concluded, looking ahead to the front of the column.

"Water up ahead," Joel Benchley announced as he trotted along the wagon train. " 'Pears there's enough to last a while. We'll circle up around this seep basin and rest a couple of days."

"That's good news," Jim Andrews declared, unwilling to admit the amount of pain his wound actually caused him.

An hour remained of daylight. Cooking odors filled the area around the encampment that circled the spring. Folks relaxed and asked once again to hear the tale of Lone Wolf's magic and the battle that had ended the Paiute threat. Ian Claymore had been fussing with a few more of his deadly bombs and went to set them out along the most obvious route of approach by which anyone might attack the camp. He placed them carefully, using the fuse-igniter system that had worked so well at the Paiute village. It was much better than guessing fuse lengths. He had barely returned to the circle, intent on a full meal, when the distant pounding of hoofs could be heard.

"Someone comin' in a big hurry," Joel Benchley announced as he squirted out a brown stream of tobacco juice.

"Indians, do you think?" Martha Simmons asked anxiously.

"Don't reckon so. If they be, they would most likely be Pimas or Yumas. The Pimas are all-right folks. Yumas can tend to be a mite warlike, though not likely so, this far from their home grounds."

While they talked, the thunder grew louder. Over a rise a short distance from their camp came what appeared to be feathered bonnets. Whoops and cries followed. The riders' mounts came into view.

"It's Injuns, all right," Jeeter Jenkins confirmed. "An' they don't look all that friendly."

"Get your weapons and get ready," Joel advised. "Rev'ran', you got them nasty things of yours planted?"

"All ready, Joel."

"We may be needin' 'em."

Puffs of smoke appeared from the charging men when they came within fifty yards of the encampment. Rebecca and Lone Wolf exchanged troubled glances. Surely the Paiutes hadn't gone back on their word? — Eagle Cloud had been more than a little impressed by the demonstration. Men and women, accustomed now to fighting for their lives, went routinely about readying their weapons, checking on ammunition, and

110

taking aim.

"You boys with the Springfields, give 'em a little somethin' ta welcome 'em, what say?" Joel drawled.

A dozen of the big civilian-model Springfield infantry rifles opened up. Huge 500-grain slugs sped downrange. A horse reared. It squealed in mortal agony, the sound ever so much like that of a human, before it crashed to the ground, pinning its rider. Two men whipped away into the dust cloud that trailed the attackers, their chests smashed by the deadly bullets.

Ian Claymore yanked the first cord, attached to the most distant of his bombs. It went off with a fearsome roar. Three more horses went down, riders and animals riddled with shards of tin and misshapen pistol balls. Their shock overcome, the remaining unknown enemies began to return fire.

Slugs snapped through the air above the heads of the defenders. Arrows thudded into the sidewalls of two wagons. Ian jerked the second cord.

An eardrum-bursting explosion followed.

Five men, screaming in agony, fell from their horses. The badly mutilated creatures bucked and squawled until they, too, slumped to the desert floor in finality. Rifle fire crackled along the curve of the wagons. Powder smoke and dust hung heavily over the grisly scene being acted out.

"Give 'em another one, Rev'ran'," Joel bellowed over the fury of battle.

When the third Claymore bomb went off, the attack ended entirely. Streaming tails of their horses pointed at their intended victims, the unidentified enemy raced away to the protection of the rise over which they had come.

"Hold fast," Joel advised. "They may come back."

Half an hour passed with no sign of a renewed

attack. When scant daylight lingered in the west, Rebecca Caldwell, Lone Wolf, and Jeeter Jenkins stepped out from behind the protective wall of wagons and walked toward the nearest corpses. Lone Wolf bent low and rolled one over.

"I don't believe this," Rebecca exclaimed, echoing everyone's thoughts.

"By damn if they ain't white. Least this one is," Jeeter declared.

"Let's look at the rest," Lone Wolf suggested.

Each went to a separate body, bent, and peered closely. "This one, too," Jeeter announced.

"So's mine," Rebecca answered.

"Same here."

"What do you think . . ." Rebecca questioned for them all.

"Hard to say," Lone Wolf mused. "White men done up as Indians. And why did they attack us?"

"Must have been trailing along all day," Rebecca suggested. "What reason would they have, though? It's a bit of a mystery, that's for certain."

Face nearly black, suffused with blood, eyes bulging in his fury, Roger Styles leaped from the heavy, oak captain's chair. Those seated with him at his usual table in the Crystal Palace, recoiled, gape-mouthed at his sudden rage.

"What was that you said?" Roger bellowed, even his tongue appearing purplish in his rancor.

"Eagle Cloud ain't gonna have any war, Mr. Styles. He's even sent some sub-chiefs here to Virginia City with a white wampum belt of peace. There was a big to-do up at the camp. That's when the boys got kilt. All of 'em, Mr. Styles."

A young man stood before the gathering, nervously twisting the brim of his dust-grimed, Montana Peak Stetson. "Doake, Gage, and Cord. All wiped out in the fight that followed. If I hadn't been tendin' the wagon mules, I'd'uv got it, too."

"The . . . fight . . . that . . . followed *what*?" Roger shouted, his distorted features pressed close to the cringing youth.

"This medicine man from the Crow. He come in with some white folks and demanded the release of these captives and made some big magic."

"What sort of magic?"

"Well, he floated in the air above where he was supposed to sit. Scared the liver right outta that kid that Star was teachin'. I heard about that one. Then he walked on fire. Made some trees get struck by lightning."

"Bullshit."

"No. I was there, Mr. Styles. I saw that with my own eyes. Funny thing. He had yellow hair and gray eyes. Didn't look Injun at all."

Ice seemed to coat Roger's skin. He shivered involuntarily and worked his mouth for a moment before words would form. "Yellow hair? Gray eyes? A Crow? Did he have a woman with him by any chance? A white squaw?"

The young hardcase blinked. "Sure as skunks stink, he did. How'd you know that?"

"Was she done up in Sioux clothing?"

"I-I wouldn't rightly know. She had on a white elk-hide dress decorated with a lot of beads, black braids, and blue eyes."

Worse than having his involvement with Eagle Cloud being revealed before these gentlemen of Virginia City, Roger considered this unwelcome news to

113

be far more terrible. Rebecca Caldwell.

"Goddamn her!" he raged. "Rebecca Caldwell. She's plagued me for a long time now. Years, it seems. How did she know? How did she and that bastard Baylor—Lone Wolf, he calls himself—find out about what was going on?"

"None of 'em ever mentioned a word about you, Mr. Styles," the nervous gunslick stammered. "They didn't even know we was there until the showdown, when the Paiute shaman tried to get them killed. Doake an' the rest joined in. God, it were a slaughter.

"Weren't but five of them, one a woman, against maybe twenty-five warriors, Doake, an' the boys. They waded in, though, and kilt dang near all of 'em."

"The thing is, my inexperienced lad, that one of those five was *Rebecca Caldwell*. She has been behind my undoing for more times than I care to count. She oughtta be roasting in *Hell* by now, or flat on her back under some Oglala buck where she belongs. But no. She's got to come to Nevada Territory and mess into my carefully made plans. Get out of here. Looking at you makes me sick." Roger turned his wrath on the others at the table. "You, too. All of you get out. I can't stand the sight of you."

"Y-you m-mean," Wendell Porforey quavered uncertainly, "that you actually had something to do with these Paiute raids? I mean . . . well, certainly . . ."

"Get out of here!" Roger fairly shrieked, his nose an inch from the startled banker's face.

Oh, damn. Oh, damn, damn, damn. He'd have to pull out, leave quickly before too much got said around. Virginia City had a reputation for being quick with the rope and the gallows trap. He'd get his money from the bank, take the next Butterfield stage to Yuma, then on to the coast. San Diego, perhaps. A prospering town, he'd heard. That Alonso Horton knew how to promote. Might be something promising for him there, Roger calculated as he hastened toward his room to do a hurried job of packing.

Chapter 13

Bright, blue sky, lower temperature, and little wind helped to refresh the weary journeyers. Unfortunately, it didn't give them any satisfaction regarding the mysterious group of whites who had attacked them the previous night. Rebecca Caldwell commented on it to Ian Claymore.

"I can't make any sense out of it. If they were ordinary outlaws, why dress up as Indians?"

"Such things have happened in the past," Ian told her. "Back in the 'Fifties, immigrant trains using the Utah Trail reported being attacked by whites masquerading as Indians. The most notorious of those was the Mountain Meadows Massacre. In one instance, Kit Carson, although an old man and ailing at the time, came to their aid. Another time they made it to Bent's trading post and fort with only two wagons lost."

"Who were these 'white' Indians?"

"No one knows for sure. There was a lot of speculation at the time. Some of it rather nasty."

"How's that, Ian?"

"Some of the survivors swore that they recognized

among the pretend-Indians men who had sold them supplies in Salt Lake City. It didn't seem likely. Those folks are close and clannish, but that sort of thing . . . well, it didn't fit. Then, after another such raid, the attacks stopped."

"Where did you learn about all this?" Curious, Rebecca wanted to know, on the chance it might provide an answer to their own situation.

"At school back East. The story is made a big thing of there."

"Now it's happening again . . ." Rebecca speculated.

Men worked grooming their teams, and the relaxed atmosphere around the pool formed by the spring speeded recovery for everyone. Although troubled by recurring dreams, the returned captives fared well also. Only Toby Andrews showed signs of discontent. In the late afternoon, Rebecca found him skipping stones across the small body of water.

"What's the matter, Toby? You look a little down."

The slender youngster shrugged. "Oh, it's just that there aren't any kids my own age to pal around with."

"I see. It can be kind of lonely for you, I suppose. You could be helping mend harness or something like that," she suggested.

"I've already done that. And gathered wood, filled buckets of water, helped Mr. Benchley fix a kettle of son-of-a-bitch stew. Ain't much I haven't done — except have a little fun."

"There'll be children where you're going."

"Yeah. Only they won't know me and I won't know them. Who wants to go to San Diego anyway? We was supposed to go to Oregon. Got relations there."

"San Diego's a growing town. It won't be so hard for you."

Following the Paiute attack and the disaster it caused, added to the time lost, the decision to turn south had been a natural one. She and Lone Wolf had been headed that way anyway, as had the Reverend Claymore. It had taken little discussion to convince everyone. All, apparently, except Toby Andrews.

Toby shrugged again and sighed. "Thanks, Miss Rebecca. Maybe you're right." He flung a flat rock that managed five bounces before striking the far bank.

"That's good, Toby," Rebecca enthused.

"I could do better if it was wider. I gotta go now." The lad turned and raced away, toward his father's wagon.

Food aromas filled the air as the sun sank toward the purplish saw-tooth mountains to the west. Spirits had lifted greatly. Even the soreness had diminished to a persistent itch along Rebecca's left side. Jeeter Jenkins began to play on his harmonica and Hester Claymore joined him on the mandolin.

"Another day of this and we should be able to double our distance," Rebecca speculated to Joel Benchley.

"That's the way I figger it, too, Missy. With you an' Baylor—ah, pardon me, Lone Wolf—scoutin' for us, we can roll inta Yuma in about five days' time. Then it's ferry 'em across the Colorado and on to San Diego."

"You make it sound so easy," Rebecca replied wistfully. Far too often she had learned that *easy* solutions were the most hard come by.

"Riders comin'," Rafe Baxter called out. He had been stationed to watch the approaches to the camp. "Slow, this time, and they look to be wearin' ordinary clothes."

Several men reached for their rifles and Lone Wolf trotted to where Rafe crouched below the lip of a small ridge. Strain once again assailed the travelers. Silence filled the encampment.

"Hello at the camp!" a voice hailed a few minutes later. "Can we ride in?"

"Who are you?"

"M'name's Osborne. We're from a small community over to the west in those hills. We saw your fires and decided to swing past this way."

"Ride on up a ways, Mr. Osborne," Rafe commanded.

Horse and rider appeared over the rise, followed by three other mounted men. One wore severe black. Boots, trousers, coat, and dome-topped hat. Osborne, in the lead, exposed brown boots and whipcord trouser legs below a stained white-linen duster. He sported a low-crowned hat of good quality.

"Where's this here town you're talkin' about?" Joel Benchley inquired as he came forward.

"Hollisboro. Won't find it on any maps, I suppose. We're a religious community. Been in our special valley for comin' on five years now. We were on our way home when we spotted the smoke an' all."

"You four all there is?"

"Yes."

"I'm Joel Benchley, more or less captain of this train, since when we was hit by Paiutes. Ride on in and step down. Might as well join us for victuals an' spend the night."

"That's mighty kind of you, Mr. Benchley. Did you say the Paiutes attacked your train?"

"That they did. That was a far piece north of here. Kilt more'n half our number, ruined a bunch of wagons. We're headin' south now. Passes would be closed before we could make it through the mountains."

"You're right about that," Osborne agreed as he walked his horse down toward the circle of wagons. His silent companions followed behind. "Odd that the Paiutes got stirred up by some powerful leader, then stopped raiding altogether."

Joel grinned and gestured toward Lone Wolf. "We, ah, sort of had us some powerful medicine of our own

119

along. Convinced 'em that peace was the better way."

Osborne looked incredulous. "You mean this few people ended the Paiute threat?"

"In a way, you could say that. Supper will be ready shortly. There's good, sweet water over there for man and critter alike. You can slosh off some of the dust and be ready in plenty time."

Following the meal, talk came around to the most recent event. Rebecca opened the subject with a direct question to Robert Osborne.

"Considering that you live close-by to this area, have you ever encountered any stories concerning white men dressed as Indians and attacking travelers?"

Osborne's eyes slitted a bit, though he breathed easily as he answered, "Do you refer to those incidents that happened some twenty years ago?"

"No," Rebecca answered emphatically. "I mean right here and now. We were attacked in just that manner yesterday. Some fifteen to twenty men."

"Ummm," one of those with Osborne muttered. "How was it you survived?"

"We'd fought the Paiutes three times, remember?" Jeeter Jenkins snapped back. "We'd, uh, developed some skill at standin' off Injuns. Fake ones were even easier."

Stroking his receding chin, Osborne turned his soft brown eyes on Rebecca and spoke in his mild voice. "It's unfortunate, of course. The Good One seems to have left a great deal of mischief for the Dark One to lead man into. There have been a few such misfortunes in this area of late, I have to admit. In fact, we have some of the survivors living in our community now. The One saw fit to deliver them into our hands and we've been caring for them since."

"They're still suffering from wounds, then?" Rebecca inquired.

120

"No. Most have recovered satisfactorily. Ours is a place of peace. A contemplative refuge in the wilds of the mountains. Those whom we saved from the depredations of these marauders have chosen to live among us as brothers and sisters."

"Father Hollis has a way with healing the body as well as the soul," Seth Fallon remarked. His face serene, his eyes seemed to glow with holiness.

"Oh, you're a Catholic community, then?" Ian Claymore asked.

"Definitely not!" Fallon snapped, an edge of anger in his voice. "Those *idolaters*. Pagans pretending to be Christian, that's what they are."

"What denomination are you, then?" Ian pursued.

"We, ah, have our own way to, ah, salvation," Robert Osborne replied.

Considering that a bit evasive, Ian made to press the point. Rebecca's light touch on his arm stopped him.

"I'm sure we all differ slightly in such matters," Rebecca smoothed. "Take Lone Wolf there. Although raised a white man, he adopted the ways of his Crow captors. He sees the Deity as the Great Spirit. What do names matter, so long as one is devout?"

"Amen to that, Sister Rebecca," Osborne breathed out. "I've been thinking about something, since you mentioned this attack. There may be a great deal more of these outlaws dressed up like Indians. It could happen that they attack you again. In light of that possibility, why doesn't your wagon company come along with us to our valley? At least for a while. Until these disorders can straighten themselves out."

"That's a generous proposal," Joel Benchley responded. " 'Cept we've gotta press on to Yuma."

"Really. I insist. It's the safest way. Our harvest is nearly in. In a matter of a week or so, we can spare enough men to safely escort you on to your destination."

Rebecca smiled. "You're making it hard to refuse. A lot of these folks are tired of fighting. That's why we stopped at this spring in the first place, to take a long, sorely needed rest."

Osborne brightened. "Then consider it decided. We can all leave in the morning."

After the informal gathering broke up, Rebecca walked away a distance with Lone Wolf. "There's something about that Osborne that reminds me of Roger Styles. A sort of sly sliminess."

"Hummm. I don't have him on the top of my favorites list, either. I'd rather head on south and take our chances."

"So would I. I don't think Ian is overly impressed with Osborne, either. I wonder what sort of place this valley of theirs can be?"

Lone Wolf snorted. "It looks like we'll find out in a couple of days or so. No one objected but you and Joel."

Jostled and jolted along the rough road that angled through Nevada Territory toward Yuma, Arizona Territory, Roger Styles took scant comfort in the fact he had managed to acquire a considerable sum from Porforey's bank before his hasty departure. Rebecca Caldwell again.

Where would she be now? She must have had some idea he had been involved. Why else? He had tormented himself with the same questions since word of Eagle Cloud's defeat and refusal to carry out the plans for war. Why continue them now? Dust billowed inside the mudwagon coach, despite the rolled-down leather and canvas covers on the sides. The drivers knew the road, or at least every bump in it, so they traveled at night.

Roger's days had hardly been disrupted by this routine. Up late most nights, the hours didn't matter. The coach would make its infrequent stops to change horses, the passengers dismounting and taking refuge in the way station from the hot sun, until a few hours before darkness came. Then off again for a rattling, bone-shaking ride through the darkness until some three hours after sunup. Every mile, Roger thought of Rebecca and cursed her name. He'd wait in Yuma. Perhaps she would also be moving southward. He might catch her there. Bring an end to all this.

Yes. A sweet proposition to contemplate. Corner Rebecca Caldwell and kill her. Then he'd not be bothered again.

Chapter 14

Birdsong filled the welcome cooler air of the mountains to the west of the spring. It had taken another full day for the slow-moving wagons to reach the range and begin an ascent through a narrow pass indicated by their new guides. Sand and cactus dominated the terrain for some while. Then, as the caravan rose higher into the enfolding hills, pines and meadow grass began to appear. Near the end of the journey, the path became so constricted that it barely permitted passage of the wagons. After topping the final rise, a spectacular vista opened to the weary travelers.

Lush and inviting, a large teardrop-shaped valley spread before them. A wide, meandering creek, clear and blue, wended its course through the heart of the rich country. Fields of ripened grain reflected a golden hue, while already-harvested squares and green pasture created a wholesome-looking patchwork that offered welcome. Small houses and barns dotted the landscape and, in the distance, a cluster of buildings denoted a village. Some of the uneasiness that had been troubling Rebecca Caldwell left her when she gazed upon this placid scene.

"You certainly have a beautiful valley, Mr. Osborne," she remarked.

"It's much like the Garden must have been before the Fall. Pride is a sin, but we must admit to feeling a certain sense of, ah, satisfaction in what has been accomplished here."

"Rightfully so," Ian Claymore injected. "The effort of taming such a wilderness must have been monumental."

"In terms of physical effort, yes. Yet, the Spirit lifted us and lightened our burdens. We'll ride on in now and meet Father Hollis."

Rebecca began to notice some disconcerting contradictions the closer the column came to the village at the far end of the valley. Men laboring in the fields would pause in their efforts and stand silently to watch the wagons pass. None lifted a hat or waved an arm in greeting, though. A heavy silence pervaded the valley. Then, as they neared the outskirts of the small community, Rebecca heard a low murmuring, some sort of chant or singing. Her curiosity must have shown on her face.

"That's the women whose calling it is to fashion our clothing. They sing praises to the One while they work. Everyone here is joyful in the Body of the One. After a while, you'll enjoy singing His praises, too, I'm sure."

Rebecca pondered that in silence for a moment, doubtful that she would ever do so or that they would be here long enough for it to become necessary. In a spacious central square, dominated by a large meeting house and what appeared to be small factories of varying sorts, the wagon train halted.

"Father Hollis," Robert Osborne called out. "We have returned with pilgrims seeking solace."

Not quite the case, Rebecca thought. Her unease, fully revived now, continued. She watched the tall double doors of the meeting house open. After a dramatic pause, a man stepped out onto the stoop. He appeared to be about forty, tall, well-built, with deep-set, burning eyes. His thinning, mousy-brown hair, partly hidden by a brown cowl, receded dramatically on the sides, leaving a marked widow's peak. Despite her caution, Rebecca felt a strange fascination with the robed leader of this unusual sect.

"Welcome to Hollisboro," his soft, sonorous voice declared. "I'm Fairgood Hollis, Father Hollis, a teacher to these souls who have gathered in the Body of the One."

"You are their leader, then?" Ian Claymore asked.

"No," Hollis denied. "We have no leader but the One. I merely instruct and guide. Who might you be, sir?"

"I'm Ian Claymore, a minister of the Presbyterian Church."

"Ah!" Hollis exclaimed, as though taken by total surprise by the suggestion of orthodoxy. "A laborer in the vineyards of the Lord. Well, your doctrine may be flawed, but I'm sure you serve with diligence and dedication, Reverend, ah, Claymore. Elder Robert, see to accommodations for these fine folks and have some of the younger boys care for their livestock."

"Yes, Father Hollis."

Later, after housing assignments had been made — the single men being accommodated in a bare, barracks-like building next to the meeting house, women and children placed in homes of Hollis's followers — Rebecca met under a large oak tree to talk with Lone Wolf and Ian Claymore.

"Did you notice there were not any stores as such?" she inquired.

"You're right," Lone Wolf answered. "There's a blacksmithy, a wheelwright's, and harness shop, the singing seamstresses, but no general mercantile, obviously no saloon—no other businesses."

"A communal way of life," Ian remarked. "All labor for the general good. There are other such sects, as you know. The Amish are probably the best known. In the early days, the Mormons practiced a form of this also."

"The people stink," Lone Wolf said simply.

"Yes," Rebecca replied, nose wrinkled. "I noticed. It's as though they haven't enough water for bathing. Yet, there's several springs around and the creek. I wonder why that is?"

"Hard telling," Ian answered. "It could be a carry-over from old European customs. Or some peculiar taboo of this sect. Whatever the case, we won't be here long enough to worry about it."

"You feel the same, then?" Rebecca asked, a tiny ring of anxiety in her words.

"For a place that's supposed to be so full of joy, these people are a bit on the dour side."

"Ian had touched upon something that had first revived Rebecca's foreboding. "Do you think there's any danger for us here?"

Ian smiled fleetingly. "Danger can be anywhere. I'm sorry, Rebecca, that was a flip answer. You sense it, obviously. As does Lone Wolf. Joel Benchley is acting like he had his trousers full of chiggers. I'm not so certain these folks mean us ill, yet I can't shake the feeling all is not as it seems."

"We'll have to wait and watch," Rebecca responded. "Watch rather closely, I'd say."

"*Hello*." The single word was tenuous, shy, even nervous. It came out a great deal like the small boy who said it. Hands in the waistband of his homespun trousers, he kicked a round-toed shoe at a pebble at the side of the road.

"Howdy. My name's Toby. Toby Andrews." The affable boom of Toby's voice seemed unusually loud in the dominant silence of the valley.

"I . . . I'm Damon Trent. You came with the wagons?"

"Sure. Didn't you see us ride in?"

"N-no. I'm, uh, under discipline again. I ain't even supposed to be talkin' to you."

Toby's brow wrinkled. "What do you mean?"

The skinny, tow-headed youngster fixed big, deep-blue eyes on Toby's face. "When you do something bad, Father Hollis calls a Conference With the One. All the adults attend. They pray a lot and sing a lot and it's supposed to be how the One tells them what's to be done to whoever is supposed to have been bad. Usually they do a lot of screaming at the person, slap 'em around some, even beat 'em with paddles. Also, when it's kids, we can't speak to anyone unless it's an adult who has spoken to us first. Sometimes for as long as a month at a time. I've got another week to go."

"What for?"

"I, uh, farted during a teaching."

Toby had to laugh.

Damon's lips formed a pout and his eyes filled with moisture. "It's not funny. I *hate* them. I *hate them all!*"

"What about your folks? Don't they do anything to stop this?"

"Hell, no. Not my mom, at least. My dad don't live here. Father Hollis and all the rest say it's because he doesn't care. That he don't really love me. But I know that's not true. He does. Only . . . they'd kill him if he tried to help me get away."

"Scepticism colored Toby's words. "That's sorta strong, ain't it?"

"Unh-uh. It's true. Sometimes . . . I think—you won't tell, will you?—they're all crazy." Abruptly Damon changed the subject, the nail-bitten fingers of one hand brushing at a lock of his pale blond hair that had fallen over his high, smooth forehead.

"I heard one of the wagons was driven by a boy. Was that you?"

"Sure way," Toby answered proudly.

"Gosh. You must have a lot of muscles. I ain't got any at all." He pursed his lips, speculating, then took a chance. "Can you keep another secret?"

"Uh . . . sure. What is it?"

"I've got me a secret place. I go there when I'm hurtin' a lot. You wanna see it?"

"Oh, I guess so. Where is it?"

"It's not far. A part of the creek where no one ever goes but me. C'mon."

Damon led Toby across a pasture and into a grove of mountain willows that grew along the creekbank. A sort of low tunnel, like a game trail, had been fashioned through the leaves and branches by long usage. Damon wriggled along it like a swift young deer, Toby finding it hard to keep up. At last the trek ended.

A cutback, part of an earlier course of the creek, had formed a deep pool, fed by even slower moving water. Entirely hidden from observation by the foliage, it provided an ideal spot for a young boy's adventures. Damon gestured grandly, an impish grin lighting his face for the first time.

"Here it is."

He sat on the bank and began to remove his shoes. Then he stood to pull off the suspenders of his trousers and remove his shirt. All the while he chattered gaily to Toby.

"I come here to get clean. Folks ain't supposed to take baths, but I can't stand that. I can also go swimmin' here. Some of the other boys used to come along. Then one of them got the Spirit and told. We all got whipped with paddles and put on discipline for a month. Father Hollis said if we did it again, the penalty would be death. The human body's a great sin, you know."

Damon stopped while he removed his trousers and flung them aside. "C'mon, Toby. Get outta your clothes. The water's great."

Feeling a bit uneasy, after the talk of a death sentence for disobedience, Toby undressed and leaped into the water with his new friend. Huh, Toby thought, he had always believed he was skinny. Damon was hardly more than skin and bones. No muscle at all. Oh, well, he dismissed. A friend is a friend.

The happy youngsters swam and splashed about for a quarter-hour, then climbed onto the bank to dry. Slowly, almost with reluctance, Damon began to put on his clothes.

"When I'm here, like this . . . well, Toby, it's the only time I feel free."

Toby had nearly completed redressing. "It's sure a nice place, all right. And . . . yeah, I guess I know what you mean. It does feel free here, with no one to watch you and the breeze blowin' over your skin. Too bad we can't live like this all the time."

Damon's brow furrowed and his big blue eyes grew darker. "We could, if it weren't for people like Father Hollis. Would you . . . come here with me tomorrow, Toby?"

"You bet. It's fun."

A large iron rim from a wagon wheel served as a clarion to summon the community for any event. Shortly before six in the evening, it began its clangorous announcement of the final meal of the day. Food was prepared and served in a communal dining hall.

The members of the odd sect filed in, the men serving themselves first, then the women. Whatever was left the children got to scrabble for. A short flash of disgust crossed Rebecca's face.

"No wonder the children all look starved to death," she whispered to Lone Wolf, when she joined him and Ian at a table.

Ian Claymore shook his head in dismay. Rebecca leaned close. "In an Oglala village, the old people and children receive the choicest, tenderest bits to eat. Then the warriors eat their fill. Of course, there's a great deal more meat in a buffalo than in whatever this is made of."

"I can appreciate that," Ian answered, sniffing dubiously of the food indifferently slopped on his plate earlier.

"Brothers and Sisters, let us lift up our hands to the One in thanksgiving for this food," Robert Osborne intoned from the head table extending across one end of the long, narrow building.

There followed an interminable prayer, while the food cooled. Then Father Hollis rose and began a rambling tale, apparently a "teaching," Rebecca concluded. It went on and on while the food congealed into an unappetizing and unpalatable mass. At last, the assembly was permitted to begin eating.

"Ugh," Rebecca remarked. "I'll take yesterday's cold jack rabbit to this any day."

"Get used to it," Ian remarked darkly. "I've got a feeling it's going to be more of the same, every meal, until we leave here."

Chapter 15

"Does anyone live in this godforsaken country?" Roger Styles inquired of another passenger being jolted around the interior of the Butterfield Stage Company's mudwagon.

"There's a couple of isolated ranches, a few small bands of Pimas," came the reply. "And there's some odd sort of religious folks up in those mountains."

Not the sort of place Rebecca Caldwell would be headed for, Roger concluded as he gazed out at the moonlit vista of rocky desert. "How much farther to Yuma?"

"Another day an' a night, half the next. Ol' Fen, the driver, is makin' good time on this run."

"Except that my backside doesn't appreciate it," Roger allowed. "I'm grateful for that."

Chances were certain now, Roger contemplated, that he would be well ahead of Rebecca Caldwell and Lone Wolf. Far enough even that they might never discover he had gone to San Diego. Damn that woman.

Every scheme he had set up, from the plan to control the grain of Dakota Territory through an orchestrated war to exterminate the Sioux, to his grand plan to take a fortune in gold from the MKT Railroad and blame it on the James Gang, had been undone by the intervention of that half-Oglala bitch and her friend. Jesus! On that last venture, she'd even gotten Frank and Jesse James to help her. Then, in Kansas, her sudden appearance had destroyed his rustling and cattle-sales program. That misadventure had cost him his strong right-arm, Jake Tulley. Tulley might not have been the brightest, but he had been loyal. Nothing, it seemed, was beyond the Caldwell woman's ability to thwart.

It would be different in San Diego. A port city. A growing community with a clever, ambitious promoter like Alonso Horton opening up new opportunities. Surely a man of his talents, Roger complimented himself, could work his way into Horton's operation and milk vast profits from it. Then he could concentrate on acquiring agents to seek out Rebecca Caldwell and eliminate her forever.

That dream never left his mind and he often lovingly re-examined it. Another jolt in the road sent a shaft of pain up Roger's spine. Two more days of this and he'd be crippled for life, he complained silently.

"What a lovely dinner," Rebecca remarked sarcastically to Ian Claymore after they and the others had been excused from the communal eating hall.

"Not exactly *haute cuisine*, I'll admit."

"I wonder if tonight is anything special? Or do they hold church meetings every evening for the faithful?"

"Probably a regular thing. With nearly an all-day meeting on whatever day they pick as their Sabbath. Hear that in there now? After a lot of singing, they've reached a certain peak."

Rebecca concentrated a moment, brow puckered. "Sounds like a lot of jibberish to me."

"It is. It's called 'speaking in tongues.' There's some basis for it, but most of the orthodox faiths have considered it to be something that occurred only during distant periods in religious history. Incidences were recorded in the Middle Ages and of course in the times before Christ."

"The medicine languages of most of the tribes, although slightly different, are much alike," Rebecca observed. "Those outside the knowledge of the medicine men can't understand what's being said. Is this like that?"

"I honestly don't know. It could be. And, it's possible that this group has obtained the ability to actually 'speak' in that manner. Now, tell me what you observed about their leader so far?"

A thin, hard line formed before Rebecca opened her lips to reply. "It seems to me that there's something beyond what we see on the surface here. The one who brought us here, whom Hollis called Elder Robert, talked about others who had come here as survivors of one sort of disaster or another and chose to stay. He and Hollis implied that we'd do the same."

"There's something else I sense about, ah, Father Hollis. Greed."

"How do you mean, Ian?"

"All of this is directed by him. All of it is apparently for his benefit. No one has money, or is paid for their work. The central warehouses of the church are filled with more than is needed to supply the community requirements. What happens to the surplus?"

Rebecca thought a while. "Rather than let it spoil, I'm sure they would sell it."

"Exactly. In which case, who gets the profits?"

"I see what you mean. I can tell you one thing: I don't want to stay here more than a day or two longer."

"Nor I," Ian agreed. "I don't like the way we're

segregated, one from another, either. Or that we seem to be constantly watched."

An impish expression altered Rebecca's face. "We're not watched all that closely. And it is a nice full moon up there. Do you think we could slip away to someplace private?"

A small rumble of delight came up from deep in Ian's throat. "I've been considering that very thing."

Hand in hand, they walked through the dark shadows of the village, out into the silvery illuminated fields. By mutual unspoken agreement, they headed toward the creek bank. Rebecca's heart pounded and the tightening of Ian's hand on hers told her he felt equal excitement.

Inadvertently, they discovered Damon Trent's favorite spot. Under the umbrella bower of a huge willow, they found a convenient nest of soft, dried grasses, brought by the boy to provide a place to dry off after his swimming and bathing endeavors. It also made a perfect trysting spot for lovers.

Wordlessly they removed their clothing, thrilling again at the delightful vision of each other's naked flesh. Rebecca reached out shyly and caressed Ian's chest. She felt a tingle as his skin reacted to the pleasant contact. He, in turn, gently kneaded one rosebud nipple until it grew erect from her growing arousal. They stepped closer and kissed.

Rebecca's tongue probed into Ian's mouth, exploring, tasting his sweetness. Her body radiated the heat that built within. His rigid organ pressed insistently against her lower belly, giving new thrills. Slowly, they sank to their knees. When their long, amorous embrace ended, Rebecca reversed herself and supported her upper body on her elbows.

Legs spread wide apart, she invited Ian to make love to her—to satisfy her growing need.

"Take me this way, Ian," Rebecca urged. "You'll love it. And . . . it drives me wild."

Ian was more than willing, and at the moment of contact they both shivered with delight. With a gradual pressure, he entered her.

A shudder ran through Rebecca's body. "Aaaah," she sighed softly. "More. Reach in front and take me by the hips. Then draw us together."

Ian, fired with his own passion, complied with alacrity. New charges of unearthly joy burst within Rebecca's being as she stretched to accommodate him. As he thrust deeper, she began a grinding motion, moaning slightly with each thrust. Ian withdrew and plunged again.

Starbursts filled Rebecca's head. Every nerve seemed excited by their unusual coupling. Oh, how unbearably fantastic, she gloried. Accustomed to each other, they soon developed a steady, rocking rhythm, fast for a while, then deliciously slow. The present and their surroundings faded away.

Urgency snapped back into focus for Rebecca as she sped up the slope to her first tremendous crash of release. When it came, it whirled her away to another galaxy of ecstasy.

Side by side, on the soft, sweet grass, they lay and gazed through the leafy bower at the stars and waning full moon. Rebecca rose on one elbow and bent over Ian. She kissed his lips lightly, then worked her way down his chest, over his belly, and at last to his most sensitive flesh. There she began with lips and tongue to fire him to new life.

She had little to worry about.

Her slow, gentle motion filled Ian with tingling delight. Then she backed off a bit and began to tease his sensitive skin with her tongue. He writhed on the grass and began to thrust upward with his hips. Then

136

he threw back his head and whispered in urgency.

"Now! Now! Let me have you."

Rebecca rolled onto her back and spread wide her legs. In a flash, Ian had penetrated her and she gripped his waist tightly with her crossed ankles. With powerful strokes, Ian filled her with delight beyond all previous couplings. Their happiness went on forever, binding them in a mystery of tenderness and force that melded their souls into one.

When the inevitable arrived, the transported lovers worked to prolong it a bit more, then surrendered with a crescendo of sublime bliss.

"Once more," Rebecca pleaded when she regained her breath. "At least once more, Ian, my love."

"Yes. Oh, most surely. . . ."

Only a scant three hours of darkness remained when the sated couple returned to Hollisboro. What might await on the next morning they neither knew nor cared.

Chapter 16

Ice, colder than the chilly morning air, touched the words of the prim, pinched-faced woman who confronted Rebecca Caldwell outside the communal dining hall the next morning.

"You were not in the house of the family assigned to care for you for most of the night. What is the reason for that?"

Sister Amelia Whitt had been effusive and sorghum-sweet in her greeting of the wagon-train members the previous day. Now, the hardness in her voice caused Rebecca to bristle immediately.

"Frankly, I think that to be my own business."

"Not in Hollisboro, it isn't. Where were you and what were you doing?"

"I spent a while enjoying the stars, as I'm accustomed to do. I'm half-Sioux, you know."

"I find that explanation entirely unsatisfactory."

"Let me remind you, Sister Amelia, that I'm not a member of this . . . this, ah, religion of yours. The way I see it," Rebecca went on, her anger mounting, "what I do is none of your damned business."

"Hunf! I'll have to take this up with Father Hollis."

"Discuss it with anyone you like. My answer is the same."

"Those who do not follow the rules are severely punished," Sister Amelia warned darkly.

"Oh?" Rebecca replied in an unconcerned tone.

She recalled the retributions and punishments promised her by her uncles, Ezekiel and Virgil, by Jake Tulley and his gang, and by Roger Styles. Of all of them, only Uncle Ezekiel and Roger Styles remained alive. The threats of a religious fanatic bothered her not in the least—particularly a tall, willowy one who switched moods in an instant and who was no doubt totally unaware of the mechanics and aftermath of violence.

Confronted by Rebecca's indifference and refusal to make further comment, Sister Amelia turned on one heel and stalked off toward the large, comfortable house on the other side of the meeting hall.

"Becky," the white squaw told herself, "you've just made an enemy."

Roger Styles shuffled through a series of cards he carried in his alligator-hide Blackstone bag. Some of them were mere calling cards, in a variety of names, others quite official looking. At last he settled on one, smiling slightly. A thick, all-linen-bond stock, some two-and-a-half by three-and-a-half inches in size, it bore the Seal of the United States and in bold letters bore an inscription guaranteed to impress:

TREASURY DEPARTMENT OF THE
UNITED STATES
Mister James Morton, Esq.
SPECIAL AGENT

It also bore the signatures, carefully forged, of the Secretary of the Treasury and the President of the United States. Roger placed it in a leather folder, tucked that in an inside pocket of his frock coat, and left his Yuma, Arizona Territory, hotel room for the U.S. Marshal's office.

After introducing himself as James Morton, and showing his spurious credentials, Roger launched into his prepared ruse: "Marshal, a female fugitive is believed to be on her way toward Yuma. She may be disguised as an Indian woman. Her name is Rebecca Caldwell and she's wanted for forgery of United States currency."

"I see. Odd I haven't received any flyers on her as yet," the bulky, mustachioed man behind a battered oak desk remarked.

"It was only recently that her identity became known. I've been following her from the point the trail took up in Denver. It's my belief she is traveling through the desert in this direction. Her ultimate destination is in doubt. Therefore, I will be going on to San Diego. If she does indeed come to Yuma, it is important that you take her into custody and notify me, so someone can come and get her."

"A woman counterfeiter? Odd, isn't it?"

Roger gave a depreciating chuckle. "A women's hands are smaller and often more steady than those of a man. Who better to engrave plates? And they have infinite patience, or so I've been told. If enough of her bogus money got into circulation, it could seriously undermine the economy of the nation." Roger grew serious, calling on patriotism:

"It's up to us, Marshal Warren, to see that doesn't happen. I'm counting on you."

"Rest assured, Mr. Morton, if this Caldwell woman shows up here, as an Indian or anything else, I'll clap her inside a cell within an hour."

"Thank you, Marshal. Good day. And . . . I'll certainly keep in touch."

Long, slanting rays of orange sunlight came through the windows of the Wharton cabin in Hollisboro. Ben and Alice Wharton sat in uncomfortable, straight-back chairs, facing Fairgood Hollis. Their faces held blank expressions, stunned by the information imparted to them by Father Hollis. It couldn't be, they communicated in unspoken contact.

"How do you mean that we have grievously transgressed the rules of the community and offended the order of the Body of the One?" Ben demanded.

"You allowed that half-breed, the Unsaved woman, to wander about at night. Not only the first night they were here, but every one since. Sister Amelia warned you about this, I'm certain. It is a grave error, Brother Wharton."

"She is not one of us," Alice Wharon protested. "How can we control the way she lives her life?"

"You could lock her in her room," Hollis suggested nastily. "As matters stand, the Council of Elders might decide it is necessary to place you under discipline."

The shock of his words whitened their faces. They had witnessed the humiliation and torment of others similarly condemned by the community.

"There is, however, another way that might prove efficacious to all concerned."

"What is that," Ben inquired, grasping at any hope.

"First off, we'll move the half-breed, Caldwell, to another place where she can be more easily confined at

141

night. Then, to demonstrate your faith and loyalty to the One, you can give your daughter, Ellen, to me in symbolic marriage."

Lines of stubbornness formed in Ben Wharton's face. Everyone knew of, though none dare criticized, Fairgood Hollis's desire for young women. But Ellen was still a girl. Barely turned sixteen. No. He could not permit this. There had been others, single girls and married women alike. Some had borne children fathered by Hollis. The oldest of these, now nine and ten, had come to the valley when the mountain retreat had first been established. Better than a dozen more had come into the world in the five years since, and the group was called the Band of Angels. By all that was Holy—and Ben Wharton didn't entirely swallow the guff put out by Hollis—his daughter was not going to be the next mother of a little Angel.

"Forgive me for saying this, Father Hollis," Ben began politely enough. "But that isn't possible. Ellen is . . . Ellen is only a child. Barely past her sixteenth birthday. She has hopes of, well, of when the One approves, she'd like to be wed to the Throckmorton boy, Elbert."

"Ummmm. Not the most perfect of unions. We would have to have a Council on it. Of course, her symbolic marriage to me would in no way be an obstruction to later matrimony with the Throckmorton lad. He and his family should be honored, as a matter of fact. As should you." Hollis's tone turned to one of admonishment.

"I'm surprised at your lack of zeal for this proposal. It is a spiritual honor for the girl and for her family. Considering your present fall from Grace, I hardly expected this sort of resistance."

His patience with this smooth-talking seducer ex-

142

hausted, Ben Wharton roared at the leader of Hollis-boro. "I'm her father, man! Yet, here you are, casually informing us you're going to bed with her like one would visit a common whore. No, by God. You'll not have her."

Livid with anger at being thwarted by this heretic, Fairgood Hollis rose slowly from his chair, one fist clenched, which he shook in Ben Wharton's face. His lips had taken on a purplish hue, stretched thin, and a nasty edge sounded in his voice.

"You'll regret this, I warn you. I gave you a chance. Not only a chance, but an enviable opportunity for honor in the community and you turned it down. Prepare yourselves, and your daughter, for the decision of the Elders."

Without a good-afternoon, Father Hollis stomped out of the Wharton cabin.

Another day slipped by. Afternoon came, the men and women of Hollisboro worked about the valley, bringing in the last of the harvest or doing washing. The usual *a cappella* group toiled in the clothing factory, while the blacksmith and his three young apprentices labored over the forge. Rebecca and Ian went directly to Fairgood Hollis's office shortly after the noon meal.

"We've been checking the wagons. They're in fine condition and our stock is sleek and healthy," Ian announced. "Now that harvest is coming to an end, you'll have the men to spare to escort us as Mr. Osborne promised. We'd like to leave tomorrow if it's convenient."

Hollis frowned. He made a small *moue* with his thick lips. "I'm sorry to say that it won't be possible. I have received reports of more raids by these white renegades. The danger would be too great, I'm afraid."

"Hasn't the law done anything about it?" Rebecca asked.

Hollis spread his hands in a wide gesture of resignation. "We have no lawmen as such in our community. The nearest is in Arizona Territory, at Yuma. Or far to the north, in Virginia City. The chances of either U.S. marshal bringing a posse this distance are small."

"This band of marauders seems to have created a bit of a stir," Ian suggested. "Surely they'll have to move on soon."

"Of course," Hollis agreed in a warm tone. "That's why I urge you to remain with us a few more days."

Toby Andrews curled his bare toes around the thin, wobbly limb. "Are you sure it's deep enough to dive, Damon?"

"Of course, Toby. I've done it lots of times. C'mon."

"All right," Toby dragged out.

He bent forward slightly and put his hands over his head. In a flash of white skin, he streaked down into the cool water. His fingers touched mud and he bowed himself, surging for the surface. His head broke through the spray, and he gasped for air.

"See? I told you," Damon taunted.

"Only just enough. I got my fingers in the mud."

"You're stronger'n me. So you probably went deeper."

"How long can we stay?"

"Not for more than an hour. I'll be missed."

The boys swam lazily for a while. Suddenly, Toby did a surface dive. He came up grasping Damon around the waist and threw the lighter youngster a short distance.

"I got ya!" he chortled with glee.

"You gotta watch out now, I'm sneaky."

"It's getting cold," Toby declared after some twenty minutes.

"Yeah. Let's get out."

Sunlight through the willow leaves dappled the boys' unclothed bodies as they lay side by side on the dry grass. Toby stared at the sky a short while and chewed on a stem. Then he rolled onto one side, facing Damon.

"What's it really like, this church thing of yours."

"I told you, I *hate* it. They talk for hours sometimes. And there's even things the kids aren't allowed to listen to or take part in. I don't know why my mom got mixed up in this thing, but it's awful."

"D'you ever think of running away?"

"Sometimes," Damon admitted cautiously. "I want to find my dad, live with him instead."

"Why don't . . ." Toby began, planning as he spoke. "Why don't you hide out in our wagon when we leave? You could get away and maybe find your father. Or you could live with my dad and me for a while."

"They'd come after me."

"Ian, ah, Rev'rand Claymore's got some nasty tricks up his sleeve. You'd be surprised. Think it over, Damon. He'd not let you be taken back. Miss Rebecca'd not either. Uh, we'd better get dressed, huh?"

"Yeah, suppose so," Damon replied regretfully. He'd been serious when he told Toby the only time he felt free was down here at the creek.

Silently, their young minds working excitedly on the miracle of escape, Toby and Damon trudged through a pasture back toward Hollisboro.

"We'd better be careful they don't catch us down there," Damon said in a near-whisper. "I've been thinkin' about it lately. Someone's bound to get suspicious."

"That's another good reason for you to come with us. No more of this paddlin' and all that stuff."

"I . . . I'll think about it, Toby. Do you really believe it could work?"

"We won't know if we don't try."

Eyes alight with dawning hope, Damon gave a slow, contemplative nod.

"You have to change your ideas concerning these outsiders," Sister Amelia Whitt declared strongly.

"Oh? Why is that?" Father Hollis inquired in his soft, persuasive voice.

"There are too many of them. They are too worldly and lastly, too well armed. Were we to attempt to detain them as we've done before, I'm positive it would fail. They are willing to fight. Even that minister, Claymore."

"I agree," Brother Will Thackery said flatly. "They have been attacked repeatedly and survived. Partly because of a bomb developed by Claymore."

"A man of the cloth making a bomb?" Hollis returned with a patronizing chuckle. "I hardly think so."

"It's true. You've not seen it or heard of it before, but the effect is devastating."

"Can't we win them over?" Hollis suggested.

"Some, perhaps," Amelia allowed. "At least among the women. But they talk of leaving. How could you prevent it?"

"There could be another Indian attack."

"Not the Paiutes," Thackery put in. "They've scattered back to their usual family-band areas. And I doubt if enough of the white renegades could be assembled to withstand any determined resistance."

"Humm."

"Not very enlightening, Fairgood," Amelia snapped. "There's one among the women far more dangerous than some of the men. That half-breed, Caldwell."

"Aaah, yes. Rebecca Caldwell," Fairgood Hollis drawled in a tone that held much more the opposite of enmity.

Chapter 17

"You know, you're really a most lovely young woman." The mellow tones of Fairgood Hollis's voice came from behind Rebecca Caldwell as she stood under a large white oak at the edge of the central square.

She turned, surprised. "W-why, thank you. I hadn't expected that your duties would allow you much time to consider a few visitors."

Hollis produced a warm smile, his deep-set, mesmeric eyes glowing with an inner fire that Rebecca read as more than religious zeal. She'd seen that look plenty of times before. Lots of men had wanted to get a hand up under her skirt. Many had succeeded. But the leader of a sect, who forbid nearly everything? He broadened the beaming expression into an unmistakably lustful smirk.

"I've always time to admire beauty," Hollis told her.

His voice awakened a feral instinct. Fine hairs raised at the back of Rebecca's neck and a tingle of warning ran along her spine. Hollis had the hots for her. In a big way, she noticed when she observed a growing bulge in his trousers. Not any subtlety here. She'd been in Hollisboro long enough to have heard about the Wharton girl and Hollis's "Angels."

"Your proper place is here with me and my flock," Hollis went on, his commanding eyes working to cast a familiar spell. "Why, you could be the brightest star in my crown of precious jewels."

"Jesus, they say," Rebecca answered coldly, "wore a crown of thorns."

"*I* serve the *One*. Don't mock me, you get-of-two-races. For all your prettiness, you could still be scourged for the sin of your parents. Terrible consequences can come should you refuse your proper destiny."

"What destiny is that?"

"Why, to purge yourself of your ancestral impurity by joining with the other women of the community as mothers of a whole, new, untainted race of people."

"Pardon me, but you *are* making a joke, aren't you?"

"I never make light of such an important matter."

"Who is to father this marvelous new race?"

"Myself, of course."

"Oh! Oh-ho! Now I've heard it all." Anger quickly replaced Rebecca's strained humor.

"My first husband—and yes, I consider Four Horns to have been rightfully and properly my husband—was a far better man than you'll ever hope to be. You're a sorry, petty little man, *Father* Hollis, cursed with an insatiable lust. It matters nothing that you hide your unnatural appetites behind a lot of religious hocus-pokus. I wouldn't go to bed with you if all other men on this earth were to be made into geldings."

Rage suffused Hollis's face, then drained it to lividity. "You *dare* to speak to me like that?"

Rebecca's thoughts turned once again to the .38 Baby Russian in the beaded pouch at her waist. A lot of men had died because of that small Smith and

Wesson revolver. Yes, she'd dare that, and more.

"In the future, *Father* Hollis, keep your distance from me. I doubt that you know a great deal about whom you chose to threaten with divine retribution. So, let me enlighten you:

"I quit counting after the seventh man I killed. I don't know how many since. The first two were Crow warriors, attacking our Oglala village. The rest have been white men. At the beginning, there were over forty men in Jake Tulley's gang. Adding my uncles, Ezekiel and Virgil, and Roger Styles, make the total about fifty. Granted, Lone Wolf did more than his share of helping me. Yet, the fact I want you to keep close in your bigoted little mind is that there remain only two, Uncle Ezekiel and Roger Styles, for me to hunt down." Rebecca paused a moment to let this information assimilate into Fairgood Hollis's brain. Then a cold, deadly smile creased her lips.

"I will not be trifled with. Keep a tight checkrein on your privates, or I'll slice them off with my skinning knife."

The violence, implied and present, in Rebecca's declaration reduced Fairgood Hollis to stammering helplessness. Thwarted, frustrated and totally in rout, he could only stomp away, his emotion-writhing face masked in the cowl of his robe.

Fairgood Hollis sat at his desk and glowered. Amelia had been right. These strangers could mean a lot of trouble. What to do? Perhaps . . . yes, a demonstration of what happened to those who disobeyed. That might do it. Another day had passed. During it, the visitors had again demanded to leave. They seemed disinclined to believe stories of more raids by the white renegades. Brother Thackery had invented a flash flood in the direction of Yuma, which had appeared to mollify them a bit.

Then the whiskered one who insisted on the disgusting habit of chewing tobacco had remarked that a few extra shovels and some willing hands could easily repair the roadway as they progressed. Damn that man, Benchley! So, then, who could be punished? Who was suitable for a particularly harsh demonstration of what might be in the outsiders' future?

Hollis took up a steel-nibbed pen, dipped it into an ornate crystal inkwell, and drained the excess against the side. Carefully, he began to make a list. One name followed another onto the sheet of creamy paper.

Half an hour passed before Hollis completed his tabulation. Then he began the difficult task of eliminating those not quite right for the public punishment he planned for the next day. Olin Farris? No. Will Thackery might have need of him. Couldn't really use any of the able-bodied men. Hollis dipped the pen again and drew a line through three names. That left plenty more. He would have to consult Amelia for the final selections.

He and Amelia talked long into the night.

Strident clanging from the wheel rim summoned everyone in the community in midmorning of the following day. Direct remarks from Robert Osborne and other Elders made it clear the wagon-train company were all to attend likewise. The people gathered in a hollow U shape on three sides of the square. Posts has been erected in stone sockets in front of the meeting house. Muttered remarks went through those assembled.

"I think we're about to be given an object lesson," Rebecca said quietly to Lone Wolf and Ian.

"Ummm. I believe you're right, Rebecca," Ian allowed. "This has all the trappings of Salem in the seventeenth century. See that kettle of coals the blacksmith has brought? Those look like branding irons stuck in the center. And those lashings on the closer post are like those I've seen in engravings of public punishment sites during colonial times."

A shiver passed through Rebecca. "Who do you suppose . . . ?" she let the question hang.

"Not any of ours," Lone Wolf remarked. "I've accounted for every face."

"This here don't fit down my craw, a'tall," Joel Benchley grumbled as he joined the trio. "Question is, do we let 'em get away with it?"

"If it's their own people, we've little to say about it," Rebecca informed him.

"This here hog-leg of mine is just itchin' to clear leather, when I see sights like this," Joel declared, slapping the worn, use-scuffed holster at his side. " 'Member back when this sort o' thing was allowed in the army. So'jer boys got strung up at the post and flogged with the cat. Damn well weren't human."

Silence covered the audience as the big doors of the meeting house opened. Hollis, surrounded by a group of three Elders and four young boys as acolytes, stepped out onto the stone stoop. He raised his arms, wide-spread, in a gesture of benediction.

"Brothers and Sisters, let us pray to the One. *Almighty One, we come to you as penitents today. For there are those among us who have transgressed against Your laws. They have been found out and are even now being prepared to face their purification, so that they may be back in the Grace of the One. Let us be truly forgiving, as You are, so that their return to the way of the True One will enlighten them.* Now, Elder Osborne, will you read out the sentences of the Elder Council, please."

"Martha Talbot. For intemperate speech that offended the One through criticism of His teacher, to be branded upon the left thumb with the initial, 'I'."

"No!" A woman cried out as a child of eleven or so was brought from inside the meeting house. "Not my baby! She's only a little girl." The man beside her shushed her protests.

Martha wore a white cotton robe that covered her to her ankles and heavy black clog shoes. Her right hand had been bound behind her and her eyes held a blank stare of stark terror. Osborne raised the paper again.

"Jamey Bettles. For using curse words, to be compelled to eat cactus leaves until you repent."

A boy of fourteen came out next, both hands secured tightly behind him. He gritted his teeth until the muscles of his jaw bulged, and a glare of defiance glowed in his dark brown eyes. From close to where Rebecca stood, a groan came from a man and his face showed a flash of fury. Jamey's father, she reasoned. Osborne continued.

"Sister Constance Hopewell. For abandoning the sacred Band of Angels to the carnal bed of her husband, to be flogged with ten stripes."

"No, goddamn you! I'll not allow it," a strapping young farmer bellowed. He tried to surge forward.

Osborne made a brief signal. Two Elders approached the enraged husband. Each hefted a thick-ended cudgel. Methodically, their faces devoid of any emotion, they bludgeoned Samuel Hopewell into unconscious submission. Angry mutters rose among the people of the wagon train. Beside Rebecca, Joel flexed his arthritic fingers and closed them over the use-polished butt of his heavy, old-style Theur conversion of the Army Model 60 .44-caliber Colt. Rebecca touched his arm lightly.

"No, Joel. Now's not the time."

"Can't think of a better," the old trail guide snapped.

"We're not ready, for one thing. Look at the others who came with us. This isn't going to have the effect Hollis expects. First, though, we have to plan, organize. Then we can do something effective."

"In the Name of the One, let the sentences be carried out," Hollis declared in solemn tones.

First came little Martha. She screamed in horror as her two jailers half-dragged her to a spot before the glowing kettle of coals. Her mother wailed and sobbed. The plucky little girl wriggled and tried to pull away. The executioner, burly Brother Will Thackery, reached out and grabbed her thin left forearm. Roughly he yanked it toward him. With his other hand well-protected by a thick leather glove, he took up the dark handle of a cherry-red brand.

Thackery squeezed Martha's clenched fist in such a manner it forced her thumb to protrude. With infinite slowness, he brought the hot iron against the tender pad. Martha howled and went limp. The stench of burning flesh soiled the fresh morning air. He jerked his head and the two custodians dragged her away.

Jamey lunged with his shoulder and sent one guard sprawling. Another Elder came forward and drove the fat end of his cudgel into the boy's stomach. Jamey bent far over, air whooshing from his agony-twisted mouth. He retched out a spew of bile and water before being tied tightly to the second of the two posts by a rod slid between his back and pinioned arms. Recovered slightly, he once more clamped his mouth tightly shut.

Thackery approached with a spiny clump of cactus in his gloved hand. He used the other to squeeze at the nerve points under the hinges of Jamey's jaw. Involuntarily the lad's mouth flew open.

"Go to hell, you sons of bitches! I hate your god-damned church," he shouted at the congregation before

154

Thackery jammed the chunk of cactus into Jamey's mouth.

Jamey jerked convulsively and he began to gag and splutter. Tears coursed down his face. After a moment, Thackery jerked the offending vegetation free. Ribbons of scarlet came with it.

"Now what have you to say."

"Fuck you! Fuck you, fuck you, fuck—*Eeiiiiee!*"

Another lump of spiked desert plant blocked off all but Jamey's scream. Thackery watched intently, hands on hips, for a longer time. When the boy's face turned purplish and his gagging, choking sounds grew weak, Thackery pulled the vicious object from the sagging mouth. Blood ran copiously, mingled with Jamey's tears,

"Do you repent?" Robert Osborne demanded.

"It hurts. Oh, Daddy, it hurts so," the boy moaned.

"Let him go. He's had enough," the elder Bettles demanded.

"Jamey Bettles, do you repent?"

Another piece of cactus loomed before the youth's red-rimmed, panic-haunted eyes. He spat blood and worked tongue and lips in a pitiful attempt to rid them of torment.

"Again," Fairgood Hollis commanded.

"No!" Jamey shrieked. "I . . . I'm sorry. I promise never to use those words again." It all came out in a liquidy gurgle while dribbling saliva turned crimson streams into a pinkish waterfall that gushed from the boy's mouth.

"Bastards," Lone Wolf grunted. "We could take 'em. Just you and me," he urged Rebecca.

"I hate this every bit as much as you do," she whispered back. "We're too far outnumbered. Those Elders have six guns under their robes. Look close and you can see. Outside of you, Joel, and I, the rest of our people are unarmed. It could turn into a slaughter."

With a resigned sigh, Lone Wolf eased off. While he did so, Thackery and his henchmen removed Jamey Bettles from the stake and dragged him off to have the cactus spines removed from his mouth and tongue. Thackery returned in moments. A glow of anticipation illuminated his small, flinty eyes. Sweat ran over his low brow and along the slab-sides of his lantern jaw. The thick ridge of bone that held his bushy brows, his slope shoulders, and overlong arms gave him a primitive, prehistoric appearance. His obvious enjoyment of his assignment made him seem even more primordial.

"Constance Hopewell," Robert Osborne announced.

"Oh, please, don't hurt me like this. Please. I promise to return to the Band. Please, Father Hollis, don't," she begged.

Three muscular Elders hustled her to the other post and spun her to face it. They undid her bonds and refastened her chafed wrists to the straps that hung from a crossbar. The scene, Rebecca thought with rising disgust, had all the makings of a crucifixion. Thackery brought out a long whip, its nine lashes knotted along their lengths, the ties coated with lead. It slithered and made a menacing, reptilian sound when he uncoiled it and gave it a trial swing. At a nod from Hollis, he began.

Constance moaned when the vicious cat-o'-nine-tails cut through her thick clothing. The first stripe had not bitten into flesh. Thackery flexed his bulging biceps and swung again.

Constance screamed and droplets of scarlet flew out toward the assembly. Several of the congregation turned away, faces pale. Most of those from the wagon train watched with frozen expressions of anger and disgust, or likewise turned from witnessing such a despicable scene. The wicked lash fell once more.

Howls of agony ripped from Constance Hopewell's throat. Several women began to weep. Those among the wagon train survivors, though they shed tears also, held angry glares on the men responsible for this outrage. The little knobs of gray glittered in the morning sunlight. Thackery applied another stripe. Rebecca forced herself to contain her fury as the terrible punishment progressed.

Mercifully, at the seventh stroke, Constance lost consciousness. "Throw a bucket of water on her," Robert Osborne commanded.

The chill liquid failed to revive the savagely abused woman. She hung slackly in her fetters. Blood trickled down her legs, staining the white robe she wore. Fairgood Hollis stared on the sight for a long while, then raised one hand in a sign of dismissal.

"Enough. She has surely learned her lesson. I hope all of this Congregation of the One has profited from this demonstration. Our visitors, too. Your conduct," he went on, talking directly to the wagon folk now, "—your conduct must be improved. You are to act circumspectly and show the correct attitudes. Your manner of dress and flagrant behavior are an abomination before the One. Dire punishment—oh, far, far more severe than what you've witnessed today—waits for those who do not submit to the Will of the One. Go now, all of you, with the blessing of the One, to labor at your tasks."

"All that cloth in her back," Joel grumbled as the four people walked away from the punishment square.

"What do you mean?" Rebecca asked.

"It's usual to strip someone to the waist who's to get flogged. Here, they've got something against nekkedness. The whip will have driven lots of fragments of cloth into her flesh. She'll be lucky if she don't die of blood poisoning."

157

"May God have mercy on her," Ian breathed out in a sigh.

He turned to look back at Father Hollis, who remained on the stoop. Rebecca turned too. When she faced the evil monster and his minions, she extended her right arm, index finger pointed toward Hollis, thumb upward like the hammer of a cocked sixgun. She paused until sure he saw the gesture, then snapped her thumb downward. Rebecca smiled while she did it.

A death's-head smile.

Chapter 18

During the remainder of the day, Rebecca and Lone Wolf sent various of the wagon folk on surreptitious missions to determine necessary pieces of information for the planning that had to be done. Following the evening meal, one in which the non-members of the community had been isolated by a pointed silence, the entire group of outsiders met while services were held in the meeting hall.

"I located our harness," Jethro Barnes declared in a low voice. "They've got it in a shed next to the harness-maker's shop."

"Good. When we're ready to go, it should be taken out around midnight before the departure," Rebecca suggested. "That way, all the teams would be ready well before sunup. The valley road is clear and easy to follow. By daybreak, we can be out of here and well on our way through the canyon."

"Why midnight?" Silas Miller grumbled. "Why not wait until closer to going?"

"Because the quarter moon will be set by then and most everyone in Hollisboro asleep. Only a few Elders will be set about as guards to deal with."

"How do you intend to deal with them?" Martha Simpson questioned.

Rebecca gave the woman what she hoped would be a reassuring smile. Unfortunately, the ice in her eyes signed the death warrants of the Elders. The gentle Mrs. Simpson raised her brows in startled realization.

"Oh. Oh, my. They've done many bad things, I know. But, don't they deserve some sort of trial first?"

"Did the Paiutes get a trial?" Ian Claymore countered in his gentle baritone.

"We know where the wagons are," Jeeter Jenkins went on, returning to the subject. "Thing is, these holy whatevers have removed most of the contents to their warehouses. Buncha damn thieves, if you ask me."

"We're going to have to travel light. Probably only two or three of the smaller wagons and the rest on saddle mounts," Lone Wolf put in. "The more of their riding stock we take, the fewer might be able to pursue us."

"Good thinking," Ian allowed.

"Will they follow us?" Jim Andrews asked.

"I think they have every intention of incorporating us into their, uh, community," Rebecca told him flatly.

"How could they do that against our will?" Liddy Freeman inquired.

"You saw their means of, ah, persuasion this morning," Rebecca answered. "The idea is to break a person's spirit, then rebuild it in the direction Hollis wants it to go. Crude, but effective."

"We got guns and we've got the reverend's bombs. I say we fight 'em right now," Rafe Baxter suggested.

"There'll be time enough for that, if necessary," Ian pointed out. "There's a lot of innocent women and children here in the valley. If the men come after us, we can take care of them easily enough."

"Speaking of women and children," Rebecca put in,

"have you noticed that there are some farms being worked by others, with apparently no adult males in the family? Where are those men?"

"My friend, Damon, says his father didn't go along with this bunch and never came," Toby Andrews remarked. "Could that be the reason?"

"Damon lives in town, doesn't he?" Ian asked.

"Yes, sir."

"I'm talking about farms, Toby," Rebecca said in a kindly voice. "Someone sowed those fields, cultivated them. Only the men who did aren't here now. A little something that has nagged at me made me make a count of those farmsteads. Do any of you recall that when we first asked Osborne about white renegades he seemed reluctant to discuss the matter, but did admit to knowing of such incidents? Well, my tally of places without men to work them comes close to the number of those white 'Indians' we killed."

Gasps from some of the women broke the contemplative silence that met Rebecca's challenging statement. Could it be true? She read the question in a dozen pair of eyes. She let the unsettling idea take root.

"This Brother Thackery seems the sort of brute who would run that kind of gang," she began at last. "If that's the case, we could be in for more trouble than we think. I don't like bringing up such a possibility, though we have to be prepared in the event it's true."

"Osborne also said some of the community came here as survivors of such attacks," Ian added. "Could they have been captives?"

"It would fit," Lone Wolf stated.

"Then I think we ought to find a way to manufacture a few more of my little devices," Ian declared.

"The dynamite's been taken off the freight wagon," Jeeter Jenkins informed them. "Put in a little place with a narrow door. Sort of an underground powder magazine. The door's locked, but there's a ventilation pipe about a foot and a half across."

"I'm small," Toby volunteered. "I can slide down that shaft and send up the dynamite."

"That's too dangerous, Son," Jim Andrews protested.

"No it ain't, Dad."

"He's the only one we have."

Rebecca's sensible remark made the elder Andrews pause to consider. His son urged his point further.

"Damon could go with me. He's even skinnier than me."

"Damon is one of them," Lone Wolf objected.

"No, he's not. He hates Hollis and his church. He . . . he wants to run away when we go. Hide in a wagon or something. Then go lookin' for his father. He'd help, I'm sure."

"Two small boys? Working without lights . . ."

"I know what a dynamite stick feels like," Toby interrupted Ian's depreciation of the proposal. "We could do it tonight. Damon can sneak out. He's done it before. Then work could get started on the bombs."

"I think . . ." Rebecca started. "It's the best answer to doing this in secret. We should do it. Can you find your friend now, Toby?"

"Sure, Miss Rebecca. Dad, can I?"

"You mean *may I*, Son. I'm sure you're physically able." His father's tone of kindly correction told Toby the answer before Jim Andrews spoke the words. "Go ahead. We all have to take risks, it seems, if we're to escape these monsters."

Filled with boyish energy, Toby dashed off into the darkness. He returned some fifteen minutes later with a thin, tow-headed youngster who looked at the gathering with solemn, dark-blue eyes.

"This is Damon. He sure wants to help."

"I'll do anything. If . . . if you'll let me come with

162

you. I know what town my dad was living in. Maybe I can get back to him."

He looked so frightened, yet determined to brave it out, Rebecca wanted to hug him, to reassure Damon that all would be well. Instead, she nodded as though making a final decision.

"You know what you'll have to do?"

"No, ma'am."

"You and Toby are going to slide down the ventilator shaft of the powder magazine and send up loads of dynamite, fuses, and fuse caps. That's so we can leave here tomorrow night or the next night."

Damon swallowed and blinked his eyes. The freckles on his lightly tanned face seemed to writhe as he crinkled his nose and stared directly at Rebecca. "A-anything. I *mean it.*"

"Good boy."

"I'm going to slip out of here tonight and scout the route through the canyon and to the southeast," Lone Wolf announced. "I'll put markers along the way and try to be back here before you make the final move."

"Good luck," several whispered voices followed in his departure.

Soon after midnight, four dark shapes scurried over the ground, bent low, to the position of the powder magazine. They located the ventilator shaft easily enough and gathered around it. Ian deftly pried off the rain deflector and examined the interior of the smooth pipe.

"Feels clear enough, far as I can reach," he whispered.

He and Rebecca produced long coils of rope and began to fashion harnesses for the boys. While they did, Damon started to pull off his shirt.

"Be easier if we did it without our clothes," the tow-headed youngster suggested.

"Yeah," Toby agreed, stripping out of his own clothing. "We talked about it and I brought along some axle grease. We'll just slide down there like a windmill pump in a well."

"All right, but keep your shoes on. There may be sharp objects on the floor," Rebecca agreed.

She and Ian helped grease the boys' naked bodies. Damon seemed embarrassed, yet excited, by the touch of her hands. He gave her a wistful, half-formed grin. Then, one by one, Rebecca and her companion lowered the youngsters down the pipe. When the ropes went slack, all they could do was wait and be watchful.

Time seemed to drag. Twice, Elders patrolling the night-time community walked past the front of the magazine. One checked the lock, rattling it loudly. *Smart boys*, Rebecca thought, when no cry of alarm came from inside. A tug came on one rope shortly after.

Rebecca and Ian hauled on the line, pulling up a bundled package of some fifty sticks of dynamite. That would be more than enough, considering the second load being prepared now. The signal that only one more would be needed was to not lower the rope. Ian held it in readiness to haul up one of the industrious lads below while the seconds crawled like spiders along his neck and spine. Another tug.

Up came the explosives. Quickly, wordlessly, Rebecca and Ian untied the bulky cargo and lowered both ropes. A long time seemed to pass, then a strong jerk on the hemp line. Both adults heaved to draw up their burdens. Though neither boy could weigh much over eighty pounds, it became an enormous task with the demands of silence and caution. At last, Toby's head popped out of the shaft.

It would be like Damon to insist his friend went first, Rebecca thought.

"We had an argument about who came first," Toby whispered. "We had to play 'scissors, rock, and paper' to see who went." His young face grew sad. "Damon lost."

Tears of love and pride welled in Rebecca's eyes. Damon had probably deliberately lost. Toby had found a true friend. She felt the pressure on the other line she held and motioned for help. It seemed forever, yet only seconds passed before Damon slithered out of the pipe. Crouched low, both boys wiped off what grease they could and donned their clothes.

"Time to get out of here. Can you get safely back into your house, Damon?" Ian inquired.

"Don't have to," Damon answered, his piping whisper filled with mischief. "I told my mom I was staying at Miz Leathers's where Toby is housed. That Toby was beginning to like the church and all, so I could help bring him around. She let me without a single question."

"You're a scamp," Rebecca declared, engulfing Damon in a stout hug, "but I love you for it. Now get off on your way. Uh, Toby what did you tell the Leathers woman you'd be doing?"

"That Damon had asked me to come stay at his place and worship the One with his family."

"I might have known. Boys. They've got a way around us adults," Ian remarked in an amused tone. "Do you have a place you can spend the rest of the night and get that axle grease cleaned off before tomorrow?"

"Sure do," Damon answered proudly. "My secret place down on the creek. Under a big ol' willow. Even have some soft grass there to sleep on."

Rebecca and Ian exchanged startled glances. Was it the same place? No doubt it would turn out to be. They wanted to laugh aloud, though they couldn't.

"Good night, and be careful, you two. Thank you both," Rebecca told the boys.

"This sure feels good," Toby declared as he lathered up his hair and passed the bar of lye soap to Damon.

"Yeah. I used to hate takin' baths. Until I came here and they said it was wrong to do so. You think I'm weird for that?"

"Naw. Just bein' a boy. Like me an' school. Now that there ain't one, I miss it awful."

That dissolved both youngsters into a fit of giggles as they continued to bathe away the axle grease in the early morning hours. The creek water felt good and they luxuriated in it, swimming, washing, and examining each other for spots they may have missed. When the cleanup job had been completed, they began diving from the branches of the willow.

"It sure felt funny down there in the dark last night," Toby admitted at last, poised on a limb.

"I know. I thought you were gonna bust my ribs when you hugged against me while those Elder bastards rattled the lock. Were you scared?"

"Naw," Toby answered blandly. Then he dived and came up close to his friend. "At least, not a whole lot."

"Me, too."

"There! There you are!" A strident female voice cut into the peaceful reverie at the creek. "Sin! Abominable sin!"

Brush crackled and revealed the pinch-face figure of Clara Leathers. "Lie and sneak around and now here you two are in the water. Are you . . . are you . . . ?" She choked off the impossible, examined the piles of clothing on the grass near the bank. "Oh! Oh, may the One forgive you! Naked! How horrible. Come quickly. I've found them."

166

Damon's mother, a thin whiplash of a woman who gave the appearance of floating rather than walking, soon appeared, along with Elder Robert Osborne and three other of the community's enforcers.

"You were warned about this once before, Damon Trent," Osborne thundered. "Which one of you lured the other into these unpardonable sins?"

"Don't say anything," Toby whispered to his friend.

"I won't. I hate them so much they'll never get anything out of me."

"We don't *need* to get anything out of you," Osborne gloated. "You're caught in the act. Filth. Unspeakable filth. Both of you. You know the penalty, Damon Trent. You'll both pay for it, too."

Damon paled. "Y-y-you mean w-we're gonna die?"

"I've been waiting a long time to get my hands on you, you depraved little monster, and now I'm going to see you get the full penalty allowed," Osborne responded in obvious delight.

Yanked violently from the water and hustled into their clothes, the two frightened boys were frog-marched back to Hollisboro. The unusual parade attracted plenty of attention, including that of the wagon-train group. They gathered around outside the meeting house.

"What's going to happen?" Rebecca asked of a woman whose face glowed with self-righteousness.

"The Council of Elders is debatin' that now. Too much sinnin' in the world, too much sinnin'. Those dirty little boys'll get their comeuppances, though."

"How do you mean?"

"Why, the Elders is debatin' on how they're to be executed. Nakedness is an abomination to the One, as is exposin' the body to wash it. They'll be hung, most like."

Incredulous, Rebecca and Ian exchanged blank

glaces that rapidly turned to fury. Another of the community spoke up.

"They could just lock 'em in a room and starve 'em to death. Be a mercy in a way. Sort of drift off and go to sleep."

"Elder Osborne favors burnin' at the stake," a third commented darkly. "So does Father Hollis."

"Don't they have anyone to defend them? No trial?" Ian scowled his questions.

"What for? They was caught guilty as sin itself, buck-nekked in the creek. Depravity is what I call it."

"No trial? No defense?" The monstrous implication of such calm acceptance of this injustice gagged Rebecca. She turned toward Ian, one hand already reaching for the concealed .38 Baby Russian in her pouch.

"Anyhow," the prune-faced woman named Leathers declared in vibrant tones, "they're gonna die for what they did."

Ian restrained Rebecca's slight hand movement. Eyes afire with the zeal of his own faith, Ian thundered across the assembled Hollisites.

"Like hell they will!"

Chapter 19

A somber group, shunned now by the religious community, met around their own cookfires near the wagons. Darkness had not yet fallen, still they had much to discuss. A decision had not been reached until late in the afternoon. Hollis and Osborne had prevailed. Little Damon Trent and Toby Andrews were to be burned at the stake the next day.

"We simply have to break them out of that little room tonight," Rebecca Caldwell told the others. "Then, whether Lone Wolf returns or not, we have to make good our escape."

"How do we go about it? I mean," Silas Miller hastened on, "I agree there's no way we're gonna let this happen to two fine little boys like them. Only, the place is guarded."

"If we can't force our way in the front, I still have plenty of dynamite," Ian Claymore offered. "What if we were to blow up their meeting house? That ought to create enough excitement to draw attention from that smokehouse where they're being kept. Then someone shoots off the lock and we let them out. The wagons will be ready, horses saddled, all set for the run for the canyon."

"You make it sound so simple," Miller groused. Then he grinned. "An' I suppose it really is. Those folks would go plain crazy. You pulled us outta some mighty tough ones before, Rev'rand, so I reckon we might as well go along. 'Less anyone else has a better idea?"

"Toby isn't one of theirs. Can't we appeal to them somehow?" Liddy Freeman queried.

"I have this brace of .44 Americans," Rebecca answered. "That's the only sort of appeal these fanatics will understand. You saw what my sixguns did to the Paiutes. Do you think I'd hesitate to use them on these people to save those innocent children?"

"B-but, you're used to violence," Liddy Freeman protested.

"You'd better become accustomed to it, Mrs. Freeman. You wielded a shotgun quite well against the Paiutes, and when the white renegades attacked, too. What makes this any different?"

"These are God-fearing folk."

"Their so-called god bears little resemblance to anything we know," Jethro Barnes informed her. His voice continued, tinged with disgust, rising to anger. "Beatings, torture, now burning at the stake. I say we kill 'em all. Every man-jack of 'em. Especially that Hollis."

A rustling came from beyond their fire-lighted enclave. All talk ceased, and suspicious eyes turned toward the sound, hands on gun butts. A man and his wife, accompanied by three solemn-faced children, entered the circle. Rebecca recognized young Ellen Wharton.

"Forgive us for bursting in on you like this," Ben

170

Wharton began in a quiet voice. "We had to come. I'm Ben Wharton, this is my wife, Alice, and our children." The introductions completed, Wharton launched into his appeal.

"We know you plan to leave here soon, by force if necessary. And that you'll try to rescue those poor boys when you go. If you won't take us all, please consider taking my daughter, Ellen. I won't tolerate having Hollis turn her into a concubine. There. I've had my say."

A strained silence held for a moment. Rebecca saw the tense resolution on the weathered face of the farmer and the fear in his younger children. No deceit here. The eldest child seemed in a state of near-shock. Rebecca's heart went out to Ellen. She spoke around a roughness in her throat, arms extended in invitation.

"And enough said it is. Of course you'll be welcomed. All of you," Rebecca said for the whole company. "How could we do otherwise, considering the despicable things that are happening here? Come, sit by the fire. We have lots of planning to do."

By ten-thirty, most of the lights had gone out in Hollisboro. Everything that could be prepared for had been done. A few minutes later the last lamp winked a window into darkness. It had been decided not to wait until midnight to acquire harness and saddles. At once, Jeeter Jenkins and three others set out to retrieve the tack from its storage place. They had no sooner left then Lone Wolf ghosted into the darkened camp of the wagon people.

"I'm glad you're safe," Rebecca greeted in a whisper. "We were given no choice but to leave tonight."

"You couldn't have better timing," he told her. "I

171

found no traces of any white 'Indians' anywhere to the southeast. I did cut some sign that indicated the men who attacked us had been out and around, also that some of the tacks led back near to this valley by a roundabout route."

Quickly, Rebecca explained her own thoughts on that subject. "Anything that could have been a grave?" she concluded.

"Two, actually. Some distance apart."

"Hummm. More mysteries. I have to tell you about Toby Andrews and his friend. Also that the Whartons have joined us. They want out of here."

It took a while, with Lone Wolf expressing disbelief, anger, and outrage, for Rebecca to encompass all that had gone on. While she did, Ian returned. He had been out preparing a few unpleasant revelations for the "faithful." He greeted Lone Wolf warmly.

"Then it's to be tonight," Lone Wolf accepted after the salutations. "Good. Another day in this place and *I* might start singing their everlasting songs."

Midnight came and the men who had gone with Jeeter returned. "We only had time to harness two wagons. There's saddle horses for everyone who can't ride in the rigs."

"That's good. We can scatter the remaining stock and create more confusion. Shame to lose the wagons," Joel Bentley replied.

"No choice, unless you want to stay here," Jeeter said for himself as he stepped in close to the huddled conference.

Jethro Barnes, grinning impishly in the wan starlight, returned a moment later. Quickly he made his report. "Food and other supplies were easy. We just stole what we needed from the holy mutterers. Plenty of water in the barrels, and all canteens are full to the

172

brim."

"You've all done good work," Rebecca told them.

She might have kissed them each on the lips, for the way they beamed.

"It's time we got started."

Silently, those assigned tasks in the escape moved off to their positions.

Damon Trent rubbed a grubby fist at the tears that still streamed down his cheeks. He and Toby Andrews sat close together, tightly bound, in the aroma-filled smokehouse. They had managed to work loose one hand each and had an arm around each other's shoulder.

"We're gonna die in the morning, Toby. I'm . . . I'm sorry I got you into this."

"We're not gonna die. Miss Rebecca and the other folks, my dad—none of them'll let these crazy people hurt us. Wait and see. They'll think of something."

"How can they? There's never less than two guards outside here. No windows. We're tied to this center post. Can't even climb to the smoke hole. We'll burn for sure tomorrow."

"You stop thinkin' like that, Damon. You're the one made me not be afraid in that powder magazine. Buck up and let's fight to the last, what say?"

Damon considered a moment. Brightened. He'd given Elder Robert Osborne a black eye before they'd been dragged from the meeting house. He'd get the other one before they went to the stake.

"Yeah," he said with awe. "We'll fight. An' . . . maybe pray you're right, that Miss Rebecca and your folks'll do something."

Disappointment smothered Rebecca's expectations when they discovered four of the Elders gathered outside the door to the smokehouse.

"No chance of doing it the easy way," she whispered in Ian's ear as he joined her.

"I didn't expect there would be," the handsome minister responded. "On the way past, I lit the fuse for the charges in the meeting house. The excitement ought to start soon now."

Bright white flashes, which quickly faded to yellow-orange, ripped through the meeting house. The roof raised upward in one piece at first, spectre of a prehistoric flying monster, before it began to disintegrate into a flutter of small, black-winged, wooden carrion birds.

Simultaneously, or so it seemed, the walls bulged outward, then became a shower of splinters, ranging from inches in size to bits larger than a man's arm. The sound of the multiple blasts rebounded around the valley. The shock wave knocked several of the raiding party flat, along with the four Elders who guarded the youthful prisoners.

"How much did you use?" Rebecca shouted to overcome the temporary deafness.

"Enough."

"Wait. Let's see what they do," she cautioned.

"Praise the One!" a dazed Elder exclaimed. "What was that?"

"The wagon people. They must have blown up the meeting house."

"What're we gonna do? There'll be fires."

"We've got to guard those brats in there, Orin."

"Not while the place burns down around our ears. You stay if you want. We've gotta raise the alarm and

174

get buckets a-workin'. That old pumper Father Hollis brought along, too."

Three of the Elders, led by Orin, rushed away, shouting needlessly to alert the village that no longer slept. Rebecca drew one of her heavy .44 Smith and Wesson Americans and eared back the hammer. She centered the sights on the middle of the remaining guard's chest.

When the hammer dropped and the big weapon bucked in her hand, she caught a slight impression through the smoke of the Elder being slammed back against the door to the smokehouse. Conscious of her short ammunition supply, Rebecca didn't use a safety shot.

"Let's run for it," she hollered to Ian.

They covered the short distance in a swift sprint. Ian yanked the corpse away from the door and Rebecca shot off the lock. From inside she heard high-pitched, excited voices.

"I told you! I told you they'd come!" Toby Andrews shouted in jubilation. "Hurry, oh hurry."

"Thank you! Hurry, hurry. Thank you," Damon Trent joined in, his tears now ones of joy.

The door swung open. Ian Claymore entered and cut the rope that bound the boys to the center post. Then he bent and freed their legs. Quickly he led them out into the flaming nightmare that had been Hollisboro. Toby ran to hug Rebecca about the waist and Damon followed a moment after. Ian took the lads by their thin shoulders and aimed them toward the waiting wagons.

"That way, boys. We'll be right behind you."

"There they go!" Robert Osborne's voice bellowed over the bedlam in Hollisboro. "They've let the prisoners free. After them!"

175

Rebecca had taken only three strides. She slammed to a stop and turned, an expression of wild delight and satisfaction on her face. Osborne rushed toward her, a revolver in his hand.

Slowly, savoring the pleasure it brought her, Rebecca cocked the .44 Smith and Wesson.

Chapter 20

Jolted awake by the huge blast, Robert Osborne had paused only long enough to draw his trousers over his nightshirt and put on his shoes. Glass crunched under his feet as he started from the bedroom. He ignored his wife's questions as he rushed through their small cabin in Hollisboro, grabbed up his revolver, and dashed out onto the porch. All around, the town had come awake. What had happened? Why? How? He asked himself the same questions others shouted aloud. Then, at the smokehouse, he saw a flurry of activity.

"There they go!" he shouted to several men milling in confusion. "They've let the prisoners free. After them!"

Osborne started running in the direction he had indicated. Will Thackery and his white "Indians" would be fighting this battle in their regular clothes or nightshirts, he thought as he strived to close the distance. It was that woman, Rebecca Caldwell. Damn her and the other outsiders. He had started to raise his pistol when she stopped suddenly and turned around.

Robert Osborne found himself looking down the large, black hole in the muzzle of a .44 Smith and Wesson American. Desperately he tried to bring his own weapon to bear. Flame lanced from the revolver in Rebecca Caldwell's hand.

It felt as though he had run into an invisible wall. Pain jarred Osborne from head to foot. His arm went slack and the suddenly heavy sixgun in his right hand dropped to the ground. Wonderingly, he looked down at the hole in his chest, blinked his eyes once, and died.

Robert Osborne's corpse hit the ground with a solid thump.

Rebecca Caldwell didn't pause to make sure of her kill. She turned once more and hurried toward where the wagons and saddle mounts waited. Ahead in the flame-laced darkness she could make out the forms of Ian Claymore and the two boys. Shouts of alarm and frightened questions came from all sides.

"She shot Elder Robert," a man's voice came from behind. "After 'em!"

Footsteps pounded on the dirt street. In a few moments, gunshots followed. Rebecca heard a bullet snap past uncomfortably close. She took time once more to turn and fire at her pursuers. A man cried out and fell to the earth, clutching his left thigh. It had been a hasty shot. Those with him paused, while Rebecca ran on.

"Spread out," someone suggested. "They'll try to get out of the valley."

For a moment, Fairgood Hollis believed that the Final Trump had sounded. The cataclysmic blast punished his ears and the ground shock knocked him from his bed. A frightened young girl, hardly more than fourteen, tumbled on top of him, screaming in terror. Hollis shoved her roughly away and stood rapidly.

Pain seared through the soles of his feet. The blast had shattered the windows in his house and the glass cut into his bare flesh. He sat down and picked the pieces from his tender skin, then drew on trousers. The naked girl shrieked in agony as she rolled on the sharp-edged shards. Hollis found his shoes and slid into them, then strode out of the bedroom, headed for the front door, which hung open, askew on one hinge. He paused long enough to arm himself.

"What the hell is going on?" he wondered aloud.

Then he saw the bedlam that Hollisboro had become.

The meeting house had ceased to exist. Flames flickered in several other buildings. The acrid odor of exploded dynamite hung heavily in his nostrils as he stalked out into the street. Men ran about, some organized to fight the fires, others seemingly disoriented and leaderless. Robert Osborne appeared from around a building and shouted something about freeing the prisoners, then started off toward the distant smokehouse.

"Brothers in the One," Hollis bellowed. "Gather around."

Men in nightshirts, others in trousers and hastily-donned jackets, stopped their aimless running and headed toward their spiritual leader. Beyond their shoulders, a gunshot sounded and Robert Osborne fell to the ground. Amelia had been right, Hollis thought. The Caldwell woman had been far too dangerous to allow to live this long. He raised a hand to assure quiet.

"You men who are already doing so, keep on fighting the fires. The rest of you spread out and locate all of the strangers. Start from here and head toward the stables and those wagons of theirs. And . . . arm yourselves. In the case of the woman, Caldwell, shoot her on sight. Where's Brother Thackery?"

"I saw him a while ago, heading after the minister and the Caldwell woman," a stout man stated.

"Send word I want to see him at once." Hollis waited through several impatient minutes until he saw the bulky, long-armed frame of Will Thackery approaching.

"Brother Thackery, gather your group of 'Indians' and lead the fight against the outsiders. You and they are the most experienced we have."

"Right away, Father Hollis. The whole lot of 'em are at the stables. They're making to get away from here." A rumble of hoofs and wild whinnies interrupted him. "What was that?"

"I think the outsiders have stampeded our horses," Hollis answered calmly, though he felt far from in control of the situation. "Hurry, man."

"Me an' the boys'll stop 'em."

"I certainly hope so."

At the far end of Hollisboro, where the hitched wagons waited, everyone stood facing the village. Features drawn and tense, the heavily armed band of travelers waited for what they knew had to be done. To get the wagons out of the valley, it would be necessary to drive through the village. They would be subjected to whatever resistance the religious community could bring to bear. Those on horseback would have it easier.

They could ride around the town, scattering the other livestock ahead of them. That served two purposes: diversion, and denying the enemy an opportunity to follow too quickly. The plan had been worked out earlier in the evening. Rebecca had allowed as how it wasn't the best possible solution. Jeeter Jenkins had then added a useful suggestion:

"Drive from down inside the wagon boxes. Those thick sides will stop most bullets. Set the mules to a run, aim down the center of the street, and hold on."

Jim Andrews drove the lead wagon, his son and Damon Trent aboard with him. Ian Claymore had also placed aboard six of his deadly bombs. Ian, on a swift Appaloosa of Rebecca's, would ride ahead and wait at the mouth of the canyon exit. There he would take off two of his devices and set them up in a manner he had proposed, though he had some doubts of the effectiveness. Jeeter Jenkins would handle the next vehicle.

Loaded into it would be more of the explosives and the Wharton family. Ben Wharton would be riding a horse, armed and more than willing to use his weapon. The third wagon would be driven by Silas Miller. The sounds of shouting in Hollisboro grew louder.

"Time to head out," Lone Wolf declared.

Those going in the wagons climbed the wheels and entered their mobile refuges. The remaining men, and some women, put their left feet into stirrups and swung astride their mounts.

"Open the corral rails and start those critters running," Joel Benchley commanded.

With loud shouts, horses and mules were driven from the corral and set to galloping across the open fields. Led by Ian, some of the riders followed after. Sudden whoops and yelps from the direction of Hollisboro informed the remaining people that an attack had been organized.

"Sound just like Injuns," Joel remarked.

"Small wonder," Rebecca replied, a faint smile on her face. "I think we've just located those white 'Indians.' "

"Roll them wagons!" Joel shouted. "We'll hold 'em here a while then follow along."

"Haay-up!" Jim Andrews yelled to his team of six mules, slapping the wheelers' rumps with the reins.

Painfully slow at first, or so it seemed to Rebecca, the lead wagon began to roll. The shouts grew louder, closer. A shot lanced out of the darkness. Lead thudded into thick oak. A yelp of alarm came from inside. That would be Toby and Damon, she didn't know which. Eyes fixed on the spot where the muzzle flash had come from, Rebecca eared back the hammer of her .44 and loosed a round.

A squall of pain rewarded her, and a man toppled forward into the firelight, clutching at his left side. He must have been moving, Rebecca estimated. Not fast enough, though. All three wagons rumbled faster now, headed into the single street of Hollisboro. They had a long and dangerous gauntlet to run. Rebecca silently wished them well and sought another target.

Like maniacal fireflies, yellow flame winked at the remaining defenders from a dozen points. Jethro Barnes threw up his arms and fell sideways from his saddle. Another of the survivors cried in pain and clutched his right side.

"Spread out!" Rebecca shouted. "Don't crowd in like that."

The riders moved their animals apart and prepared to dash away. At the far end of the line, Lone Wolf opened up with his booming Sharps. He fired at Hollisites farther down the street, unseen by Rebecca. Good. That would cut down the risk for the wagons. She sensed more than saw movement to her right, and swung her revolver that direction.

The muzzle flash blinded her for a moment. She heard muffled groans and urged Sila in that direction. Several dark forms detached from the shadows and rushed toward the mounted fighting men.

"Take aim . . . *Fire!*" Joel shouted in sudden inspiration.

A regular volley cut into the charging Hollisites.

Three went down at once. Another pair staggered off on aimless courses into the darkness. One man got close enough to grab at the reins of Lone Wolf's horse.

A meaty smack followed, as the former Crow warrior drove the sharp edge of a tomahawk into the top of his attacker's skull.

Brother Will Thackery had a bemused expression on his face when Lone Wolf removed the 'hawk and the Hollisite executioner looked upward at the man who had killed him. His eyes glazed and he sank to his knees, then face-first into the dirt. Lone Wolf shook blood and gobbets of brain tissue from the well-honed steel and slid the weapon back in place at his waist. He loaded and shouldered his Sharps once more and took aim on the center of three men blocking the street at the far end.

A ring of powder smoke formed when the big rifle boomed. It moved lazily back, obscuring the tall, blond-haired warrior. Only a brief moment passed before the burly man at the east end of Hollisboro skidded backward and flopped on the ground. His companions leaped aside as Jim Andrews's wagon plunged toward them.

Ian Claymore paced nervously at the mouth of the canyon that promised escape for everyone. The sound of gunfire increased, which only served to agitate him more. He peered toward the flickering fires in Hollisboro, and saw vague shapes moving to fight the blazes while others converged on the opposite end of town. From that distance, the human roadblock appeared as three tiny stick figures. One of them jolted backward suddenly and landed on his back. Ian heard a moment later the solid blast of a buffalo gun. That would be Lone Wolf, he thought with satisfaction. Then excitement wiped away other considerations.

The first wagon made it through the village and had broken into the clear. Only angry, fist-waving men followed a ways on foot. One stopped to aim and fire a rifle. Its crack reached Ian's ears. The wagon didn't even waver. Soon now he would be busy enough not to worry about why the remaining riders hadn't broken off and made their way to his position.

Jim Andrews heard the bullet crack over his head. "You boys stay down, you hear?"

"Don't worry, Dad. We are," Toby called forward to his father. "We're outta town now. I can see the buildings behind us through a crack in the tailboard."

"Good. Anyone else after us?"

"No. They've turned to try to stop Mr. Jenkins's wagon."

"Son, this is a hard thing to say, but do you think you could take a shot at one of them?"

"Sure. Easy. So can Damon," Toby answered with a casualness that gave Andrews a chill.

"Don't take chances, and be careful."

Toby raised on one knee and aimed his .32 Marlin carbine at the back of one Hollisite. The jouncing of the wagon bed made it nearly impossible to hold on a target, and a frown of concentration creased the boy's smooth brow. Beside him, Damon raised up, likewise, and shouldered Jim's heavy shotgun.

The scattergun slammed into Damon's shoulder with a bit more force than he had expected. Howls of pain from two Hollisites, who had been peppered with shot, rewarded the lad's efforts, though. He rubbed the sore spot a moment and readied to fire the other barrel. The Marlin made a loud noise beside him and Toby toppled backward from the recoil.

"Got him!" he cried excitedly the moment he came upright.

"Oliver Grimes," Damon identified. "He's deader'n

184

hell, Mr. Andrews."

Jim Andrews winced. Twelve years old and his son had killed a man. God forgive us all, he silently pleaded. After his wife had died, he had decided to take the boy out West to get away from the coarser aspects of civilized living in the East. What more might the boy have to endure?"

"Should we keep shootin', Dad?"

"N-no. You might hit Jeeter," the senior Andrews managed to stammer out.

"How far to the canyon?" Damon asked.

"More distance than I'd like to cover right now," Jim told the boy. "We'll be stopping sort of rough-like, so you boys hold on tight."

Angry already, a hot surge of fury burst inside Fairgood Hollis when he realized that his men had been fought to a stalemate at the far end of town. Determined to finish with these outsiders, he began to run toward the battle. Wagons came bolting at him from out of the darkness.

Hollis jumped aside barely in time to avoid being trampled by the team of the first careening vehicle. He raged at the second Conestoga as it lumbered past. He remembered the weapon in his hand and fired a shot at the third in line. It smacked into the thin wood of the seat-back and punched a neat hole. It had no effect on Silas Miller, though, who hunkered down on the bed, sawing at the reins while he hollered at the six-span of mules. Hollis watched their dash out of town, shaking with the bitter rancor of his helplessness. Then he continued.

A bullet cracked past his ear, close enough to feel the wind of its passage. Instantly he darted in between two buildings. He'd be more cautious. Slowly he worked his way through the dark, stumbling once into a clothesline that nearly strangled him. Only a short ways to go. Ahead he saw the hated yet tauntingly female figure of Rebecca Caldwell. Curbing his urges, his crouched low and made his way closer. Satisfied at last, he stopped and brought up his revolver.

He couldn't miss. Not at this range, Fairgood Hollis exulted. He took careful aim. With infinite patience he squeezed on the trigger of the old Model 60 Army Colt.

The hammer snapped loudly on a bare nipple. In his haste to bring revenge on the despoilers of his town, he had forgotten to check the loads. In front of him, Rebecca Caldwell stiffened in her saddle and turned her horse toward the pool of darkness where Fairgood Hollis lurked.

"You make a terribly inefficient assassin, *Father* Hollis," Rebecca told him sweetly. "You're even poorer at that than you are as a seducer."

She raised her Smith and Wesson and cocked back the hammer. Fairgood Hollis flung the impotent sixgun from him and raised both hands in supplication. He sank to his knees, babbling, imploring.

"Y-y-you w-w-wouldn't sssssshooo—ah, k-kill an unarmed man, would you?" he pleaded.

Rebecca hesitated. "You're right. A *man*, I wouldn't; a worthless bastard like you it would be a pleasure."

Rebecca squeezed the trigger. The firing pin made a sharp, metallic sound when it struck a dented primer. Damn! She'd forgotten to count her shots.

Hollis leaped at her with frantic energy. He clawed and bit while he hung onto her right leg with both of his own entwined around it. Rebecca clubbed at him with the unusable Smith, fighting at the same time to open the top-break weapon and insert fresh rounds. Hollis wailed, a high-pitched, feminine sound.

Rebecca struck at him again, then regained her calm thinking process. She holstered the expended weapon and reached into her beaded squaw pouch.

Against the background of heavier weapons detonating, the .38 Baby Russian made a small, popping sound.

Because of his frantic writhing and pummeling, the first slug only burnt a hot groove along Fairgood Hollis's right arm. He shrieked in agony, yet continued to smash at this object of his concentrated hatred. Rebecca fired again.

Her second bullet smacked into the top of Hollis's head, as did the third and fourth. For a moment, the fanatic leader of this vile sect held tightly to her. Then he stiffened and shuddered. Fairgood Hollis uttered a gurgling sigh as he went slack and fell away from Rebecca's horse. Sila wickered softly and pranced about, the odor of blood heavy in the air.

"Hollis is dead," Rebecca yelled at her companions. "Time we ride out of here. Split up. We'll rendezvous at the canyon mouth."

Chapter 21

"Father Hollis is dead!" a man cried out. "I just heard it."

"They're gettin' away," another Hollisite shouted.

"Go after them," an authoritative voice commanded.

"We gotta round up some horses first, Sister Amelia," came the reply.

"Do it, then," came the angry response.

Seth Fallon ran up to where Amelia Whitt stood in the center of the street. "They went all which-a-ways. What'll we do?"

"There's only one way out of this valley that they know of, stupid. Get on anything that is ridable and go after them."

Like a whipped pup, Fallon hung his head. "Yes, Sister. We will."

Outdistancing all the others by a good half-minute, Rebecca and those mounted on the Appaloosa horses reached the spot where Ian Claymore waited. One among the rest led a saddled mount for the young minister. Rebecca swung out of the saddle.

"It's going to be a while before any sort of chase can be organized. We scattered the other stock fairly well."

"You look fine," Ian enthused, unconcerned for the moment with any vengeance-minded Hollisites. "I was worried about you all the while."

"You needn't have been," Rebecca replied, weary of the battle and unaware she sounded smug and snappish. She saw the odd look on Ian's face and melted. "I'm sorry, Ian. It's only that—"

"I know. There must have been some losses. I'm sorry, too. For that, and for all you've been through. What happened to your leg?" the reverend demanded when he saw the tears in her elk-hide dress.

"Hollis. He bit me and clawed at my leg, trying to drag me off Sila."

"He could have killed you. What did you do to get away?"

"I shot him for his efforts. He's dead. Like his whole sick faith." Rebecca cleared her throat and continued brusquely. "They'll be after us soon enough. Did the wagons get away?"

"Yes."

"Good. How about your little bombs?"

"Already in place. I rigged up the detonators with instant igniters. Used a shell casing of black powder in each to insure they go. Soon as all of our people are past, I can set the trip wire in place."

While he spoke, the remainder of the escaping group rode into the gap. Rafe Baxter halted long enough to hand the reins of a bay mare to Rebecca.

"Here's fer the rev'rand. I'm gonna catch up with the wagons. Sure wish I could stay and see the fun."

"Hardly fun," Ian corrected, conscious of his calling, "—though it will come as an unpleasant surprise to our enemies."

"Good luck bein' on our side, 'course," Rafe added as he spurred his mount.

"Do you need any help?" Rebecca inquired.

"Nothing to it, now. But you can stay and we'll ride along together."

"I'd like that."

Quickly, Ian drove small stakes into the ground and threaded a thin length of stout twine around them in such a manner that it would catch the forefeet of the first horse to pass that point. He tested its tightness and nodded satisfaction. Then he came to Rebecca, took the reins to his horse, and mounted.

"I sure hope they don't send anyone ahead on foot. If he saw the twine, it would spoil everything."

Rebecca gave him a warm grin. "You like this sort of thing, don't you? No," she hastened when he started to form a protest. "It's true. And, I'm willing to bet, you're no longer so certain of your devotion to the ministry to deny it, either."

Ian remained silent, mulling that issue. A part of him didn't like the answer that rose to his conscious mind. Rebecca sensed his indecision and quandary.

"Don't feel that I'm trying to encourage you to abandon your chosen life. We've been lovers. We had some good times and shared the bad, too. I only want to point out the obvious."

Ian developed a rueful grin. "Is it all that terribly evident?"

"Ah! You know it, too. No, Ian. I don't think anyone who hasn't known you so intimately, as I have, would ever detect your, ah, reckless side."

"It's something I'll have to live with, though. And

fight at every opportunity."

"True. For the rest of your life, no doubt."

"Or at least until a comfortable old age. We'd better be riding if we want to catch up with the wagons. They were to stop halfway down the canyon."

"I'm coming with you," Sister Amelia declared when the remainder of Will Thackery's spurious Indians returned with ample horses to make pursuit practical.

"You, Sister?" Seth Fallon declared in surprise.

"Why *not* me? I can ride and I shoot nearly as well as any man here." Her voice became hard, tinged with hoarfrost. "Besides, I want to personally finish off that bitch Rebecca Caldwell."

"We, ah, haven't any side-saddles," Fallon offered lamely.

"No worry. I can ride a-straddle."

"Then we'd better be going. They're getting further away every second," Fallon advised.

"I'm aware of that, you nincompoop. Stop standing around waggling your tongue and let's go."

The posse of angry Hollistites rode out of what remained of Hollisboro at a gallop. Behind them, two-thirds of the community lay in smoldering ruin, its founder a chilling, stiffening corpse. At a steady pace, they covered ground rapidly. Fallon and Amelia rode at the head of the small column. When they neared the mouth of the canyon, Amelia urged greater speed.

"Faster. We want to be on them before daylight," she shouted over the rumble of hoofs.

She and the others still dedicated to Fairgood Hollis's perverted religion lashed their mounts with the ends of their reins and surged out of the valley into the narrow walls of the main access.

A moment later, Amelia Whitt saw the beginnings of a yellow-orange brightness at one side of the trail. The rockwall-amplified sound of the awesome detonations reached her, bursting her eardrums, at the same moment that moaning, deformed pistol balls and whizzing bits of tin shredded the life and black hatred out of her forever.

"There went the first two," Rebecca remarked to Ian. "Your new detonating system is a success."

"May God have mercy on them," Ian murmured.

"Well, these four are ready. Everyone is set to move on. We should be doing so. Daylight in less than two hours."

"Has time gone so fast?" the broad-shouldered minister asked in wonder.

"It always does when someone is having fun," Rebecca teased.

Ian had a retort ready, though he didn't use it. Rebecca called out to Joel Benchley, "Let's roll these wagons. A lot of trail yet to cover."

Slowly the reunited column moved along, bound by the walking pace of the mules who drew the wagons. Rebecca imagined that anyone left to pursue them would also be taking it considerably slower. Perhaps even on foot. Would they discover the trip lines? They'd know, when the enemy reached the midway point of the canyon. Lone Wolf had gone ahead to make sure of their route, and the lightened Conestogas made good headway. Still, time seemed to lag.

"Ian, when we reach Yuma, will you go directly to the other side of the border and your half-Indian charges?"

"I . . . uh, don't know. It would be nice if we could

have some time together before you go off to see the Pacific Ocean."

"More than nice, I'd venture. Yes. But you've been delayed now. What trouble might that cause with your superiors?"

"None, once I send them an explanation. The bad thing, though, is the loss of most of my supplies. Hymnals, prayer books, even the furnishings for the altar. Hollis and his band of ragpickers did away with them all."

"You can order more, can't you? Or borrow from other churches?"

"All of that takes time."

"Which you'd like for us to spend together in Yuma?"

"Can you think of a better way to wait?"

"No, my dear one. Not in the least."

Gradually, the horizon before them began to lighten. Dawn would come at any moment. Already a pinkish hue rose above the line of the desert toward which they journeyed. Then, with a suddenness characteristic of the barren terrain of cactus and sand, daylight popped into being with a huge red ball of sun swelling ahead of them as it climbed swiftly into the pale blue of morning.

"Oh, Ian, isn't it lovely," Rebecca enthused. "I've never seen a sunrise like—"

Wham! Wham!

"Two of the bombs went off," Ian calmly remarked over the distance-muffled sound.

"They're still after us, then?"

"I would suppose so."

Wham!

"Another one."

"How many could be left?"

"Not enough Hollisites to give us any worry, I would

guess," Ian assured her.

"We did them a terrible lot of damage before we left. Now, these . . ."

"Don't dwell on it. Some of those people had to have sense enough to realize that Hollis was mad. Surely not all of them are going to follow us."

"They can't," Rebecca replied brightly. "They'll have been lucky to find a dozen horses before daylight. Those who aren't already dead will no doubt be the ones without mounts."

"That's a grisly way to look at it."

"To me it makes sense."

By midday, the small caravan had come well out onto the desert, headed southeast now, toward Yuma. The fourth bomb had not gone off within their hearing, and no sign of pursuit could be detected. Lone Wolf scouted to their rear, using volunteers to relay his continuing negative reports back to the travelers. The solitary benefit of their protracted stay in the grim valley had been a general improvement in the attitudes and physical responses of the former captives. Ian brought this up as he rode side by side with Rebecca at the head of the column.

"Hester has mended quite well, despite her terrible ordeal," Ian observed casually.

"I've noticed. So have the others. Lucy Simpson seems the most affected by it. She's the youngest, so no doubt it will take a while." Abruptly, Rebecca changed the subject. "It's about noon. Time to give the animals a rest and have a little food."

"You think it's safe?"

"It'll be another day before we can be sure of that, Ian. Lone Wolf's messengers have been consistent in reporting no one following us. Whatever the case, they could not catch up now in the time we'd take."

"All right. I'll speak to Joel."

Unencumbered by the heavy freight wagons, the stripped-down wagon train made good progress throughout the day. By midmorning of the second, Lone Wolf rejoined the column and made his final report.

"I rode a ways up into the canyon. No sign of any Hollisites. At least, none who were alive. That last set-to with the bombs must have changed their minds about revenge. With Hollis dead, what sense would it make, anyway?"

"You're probably right," Rebecca allowed. "We have another problem, though. That run through town caused a couple of water barrels to be holed by gunshots. We're going to be short on water by nightfall. Joel isn't familiar with the terrain south of here. By tomorrow, if we don't find a spring or other source, we'll be in serious difficulty."

"What about food?"

"Not as much as we had originally thought, considering we had so few losses in escaping from the valley. It might hold another three days, though I'm doubtful."

"We could have better news," Lone Wolf regretted aloud.

When the caravan halted for the night, another discovery dampened spirits. "After all the time we've been traveling," Martha Simpson scolded herself every bit as much as she did the others, "you'd think we'd have had sense enough to be certain of our wood supply."

"I think everyone was so anxious to get away from those awful people, no one thought of it," Liddy Freeman offered by way of explanation.

"True enough," Joel Benchley added in. "But it don't lessen the effect. Particular-like with this wind whippin' up. Fuel burns faster in a big blow, as you know." Joel paused and turned about, fists on hips, considering the problem.

"You boys," he called a moment later to Toby and Damon. "There's plenty manzanita and mesquite around. What say you two scamps hustle around and bring in some dry deadfall?"

"Sure, Mr. Benchley," Toby agreed at once.

He and Damon sought out axes and hurried off into the desert in search of firewood. In less than a minute they were out of sight of the camp.

Some three hours from sundown, the sky began to darken. Joel Benchley glowered at it with a worry-wrinkled brow.

"It's getting too dark for this time of day," Rebecca mentioned to him a short while later.

"Yep. I'm figgerin' it can't be but bad news, too. Notice the wind's stiffin' up a bit all the time?"

"I've been conscious of it," Rebecca replied, thoughtfully. Then she opened her dark blue eyes in consternation. "Do you mean . . . a sandstorm?"

"It could happen. Best get things buttoned down mighty tight around here," Joel advised. An invisible spray of sand particles struck him in the face and he blinked out the stinging bits that gathered in his eyes. "An' darned fast, I'd say."

With a few shouted orders, work began quickly to protect the wagon covers and the livestock. While the adults toiled, Toby and his friend came upon a windfall treasure.

"Look at that!" Damon declared. "A whole tree, blown over. We can cut off the big limbs and drag 'em back to camp.

Uneasy, Toby looked around, then studied the sky. "I don't know if we've got time, Damon. It's gettin' dark mighty quick."

"Awh, c'mon. We can take two apiece, can't we?"

Toby shrugged. He hefted the axe over his right shoulder and walked up to the giant mesquite. Cocking his head from side to side, the youngster gave it critical study. At last he turned with a grin.

"Why not? Let's do it."

They had cut free two large limbs, the severed ends of thigh-thickness, when the sandstorm struck with howling fury. Burning, scouring grains cut at their faces and hands. Darkness became absolute.

"We're gonna choke in this," Toby declared, shouting above the roar. Immediately he regretted opening his mouth. His teeth gritted on an accumulation of sand.

"What can we do?"

"I . . . I don't know. We can't see to find the camp."

"Get down here," Damon urged. "In these branches. Take off your shirt and cover your head with it. We can make a sort of shelter that way. Hurry, Toby."

Huddled close together, their shirts supported by smaller limbs and twigs of the mesquite, Toby and Damon shivered with apprehension and wondered at their fate. They took small, shallow breaths by necessity and silently appealed for help.

Jim Andrews paused in his efforts and looked at the advancing wall of darkness, its face a-swirl with fountains of sand and debris. He looked around frantically, then turned toward the rest of the party.

"The boys? Where's my son and Damon?"

197

Gape-mouthed, stricken by sudden remorse at his forgetfulness, Joel Benchley pointed feebly toward the onrushing peril.

"Out there," was all he could manage.

"Oh, my God!"

Then the maelstrom engulfed the campsite and everyone sought cover in the wagons.

Chapter 22

Buffeted by gale-force winds, the light wagons rocked in the tempest. A seething rattle, like a summer hailstorm, scoured the boards and assaulted the fragile canvas covers. Men and women coughed and gagged in the whirls of sand-laden dust that invaded every crevice. Despite the speed of the rushing air, the storm lasted on beyond nightfall. Behind the devastating bluster came a brief rain shower, as though intended to cleanse the air and settle the effects of the ruinous flurry. Slowly, the people emerged.

"First, get a fire started," Joel advised. "So's we can check for damage."

"Easy," came Seth Miller's grumpy reply. "If we can find the woodpile."

Martha Simpson produced a kerosene lantern and lighted its wick. She held it high, to provide a wider circle of illumination.

An alien landscape had replaced their familiar campsite. Here and there, smooth mounds protruded from a uniform cover of sand that the wagon folk soon found to be ankle deep. Joel went to one hump, near the center of the triangular arrangement of wagons.

He bent and began whisking away sand, to reveal the firewood. "There. Now, let's do somethin' about those boys. I saw 'em head off . . . uh . . . *that* way."

More lanterns came into view. Jim Andrews, although still limping slightly, led three other volunteers, each with a yellow-glowing lamp in hand, out in the direction Joel had pointed. As a precaution, he took along a canteen of water.

"Toby! Toby!" he called loudly to his son.

Nothing looked as it had before the storm. The features of the whole countryside had been dramatically altered. Only reassuring backward glances at the growing glow of the cook fire kept Andrews oriented while the search went on. The stock would need plenty watering, he thought. His own thirst had become a constant torment. What about the boys? Would there be water enough for their needs? Resolutely, Jim Andrews pressed on.

"Toby! Damon! Can you hear me?"

Still no sound. Worry began to constrict around Jim Andrews's heart. "Spread out a little. You can keep track of things by looking back of us at the glow from the fire. Start yelling. Sooner or later, they have to hear us," Jim concluded.

Nothing moved around the fallen mequite tree. Nothing, in fact, remained but a large mound of sand. Toby and Damon still crouched inside a small pocket of air. Their shelter had been formed from their clothing. The interior of the little place was hot, the air already growing stale. The boys sweated in the dark and held hands for reassurance. Thirst had become the dominant factor in their lives. No water, yet they perspired freely. Soon, no air.

"D'you think it's safe to try to dig out?" Damon asked in a tiny whisper.

"What if it all caved in on us?"

"How deep do you think this sand is?"

"Hard to tell," Toby replied. "Let's not talk. Save our breath."

"We're gonna run outta air, aren't we, Toby?"

"Naw. The other folks will come lookin' for us before that happens."

"Are you scared, Toby?"

"Y-yes, I am."

"Me, too."

Three times the search party swung past the covered-over mesquite. Faintly calling, their voices gave the boys hope and they yelled in an attempt to be found. Muffled by the sand, their piping voices were not heard. The search went on fruitlessly. The youngsters grew weaker. Their condition worsened with each passing second.

Coughing in the foul air, Damon stirred, placed his feet beneath him. "I can't take this any longer. I'm gonna stand up, Toby."

"If you do, we'd better do it together."

"All right. Ready? One . . . two . . . three . . . *go!*"

Shirts still covering their heads, the boys surged upward. The gritty sand poured over them, spider legs on their bare skin. A sudden chill hit their naked chests and the heady richness of clean, pure air.

"W-we did it!" Damon spluttered over a mouthful of sand.

"It wasn't so deep after all," Toby said in awe. Their movement had revealed the uppermost branches of the mesquite, which looked like brown bones in the starlight.

"It must be after midnight. The moon's set," Damon observed.

"*Toby!* Where are you?" the welcome, familiar sound of Jim Andrews's voice came from a distance.

"Over here, Dad," Toby called back. "We're over . . . here." Weakened by the ordeal, Toby fell to one side and lay, curled slightly into a fetal position.

"Hurry. We're . . . over . . ." Damon Trent likewise surrendered to the trial they had endured.

Rushing feet, unheard by the unconscious boys, drew closer. Then a joyful shout from Seth Miller sent chills of expectation along Jim Andrews's spine.

"This way, Jim. I see 'em. They's layin' on the sand."

"Half-naked and out like someone had clubbed them," Jim observed as he hurried up. He knelt and dribbled water into the slightly parted mouths of the unmoving children. "I'll swear we were by here before. Why didn't we see them?"

"That mesquite tree wasn't here when we went by before. I bet they hunkered down by it and sheltered somehow."

"Their shirts are probably buried under all that sand," Jim speculated. He raised his lantern higher. "No. There they are. You're right, Rafe. That's what they did. Smart boys."

"We'll carry 'em to camp."

"Sure. Gently, though. They must have suffered a lot," the grateful father remarked.

With precious little water, Toby and Damon could only be wiped with damp rags. They suffered from dehydration, and Joel Benchley wisely insisted they be given only thimble-sized sips of water over a long period of time. The youngsters had regained consciousness after being doused with cupfuls of water and given a bit to swallow.

In a croaking voice, Toby tried to recount their experience. His father eased him down on a soft quilt and shook his head.

"Later, Son. You're a brave, smart boy to have survived out in that. We all want to hear, but first you rest."

An hour after daylight, the travelers began to dig out from the effects of the storm. Not a familiar landmark remained, except far in the distance a low ridge of brown hills. Their livestock suffered mightily from lack of water, as did Toby and Damon. Slightly feverish, the boys related how they had taken shelter as the storm struck them. Ian offered thanks for their deliverance. Everyone in camp made over the lads, and their bellies filled to near bursting with offered morsels. While the wagon wheels were being shoveled free, Lone Wolf and Joel decided to make a spiral search outward from the campsite, in an attempt to locate a reliable route. Before they could go, though, another problem arose.

Looking stern, her mouth puckered tightly, Alice Wharton came to where Rebecca Caldwell, Lone Wolf, and Joel Benchley conferred. "We're being punished."

"I beg your pardon?" Rebecca replied, surprised at this reaction.

"This is punishment for our defying the One."

"Oh, come now, Mrs. Wharton—" Rebecca began, to be cut off by a near-hysterical shout.

"We'll all die of thirst out here! We turned our backs on the Truth and this is our payment for it."

"Now, listen here, woman," Joel started.

"She could be right," Ben Wharton injected uncomfortably. "I didn't take much to that guff Hollis put out.

But we destroyed a church, no matter what you say. Killed a lot of folks, too. Now we're stranded in a desert with no water, little food, and no fuel. What's to come of it?"

"I'll tell you what," Lone Wolf replied. "We're going to search for a way to Yuma. We've got the sun to give us directions. This sandstorm can't have had a wide enough front to wipe out all of the trail. We're going to work outward in a spiral pattern in an attempt, also, to find water."

"Meanwhile, you and the rest of us have to make the wagons ready to travel," Rebecca put in. "There's time later for reflection on the cause of our difficulties."

"You mark what I said," Alice answered hotly. "We're going to suffer worse before this is over."

Lone Wolf and Joel had been gone for two hours. During their absence, the wagons had been dug free of sand and the teams harnessed. While the work went on, Ben and Alice Wharton had conferred and done little. They talked with their children, then came to a decision. Ben hefted one of the .45–70 Springfields and his wife drew Ben's sixgun from the holster. Together, their children quiet and pale behind them, they walked to the wagon that contained the last of the food and water.

"We'll be takin' these and headin' back," Ben informed Jeeter Jenkins, his tone edged with shame.

"You're crazy, Wharton. You come to us, beggin' to get out of that pest hole. Now you've let a little difficulty warp your thinkin'."

Ben Wharton shook his head, as though regretting his words. "Kindly step down from that wagon, Mr. Jenkins. We don't want to hurt anyone, but we will if

204

we have to."

Unseen by her parents, Ellen Wharton had slipped away and gone to where Rebecca stood, concentrating on the horizon to the east. Urgently, the girl tugged at Rebecca's sleeve and babbled out her news.

"My folks want to take all the food and water and return to Hollisboro. I'd rather die than do that. Whoever's left would kill us, I know."

"Where are they?"

"Over at Mr. Jenkins's wagon."

Rebecca started off without further urging. Others of the survivors had gathered there ahead of her. While she covered the short space, Rebecca drew her .38 Smith and Wesson Baby Russian from the pouch at her waist. At a distance of some five feet behind Ben Wharton, Rebecca Caldwell stopped abruptly when the former Hollisite raised the butt of a Springfield to his shoulder.

"I warned you, Mr. Jenkins. *Get down or else.*"

"Don't do it, Ben," Rebecca said loudly, a note of sadness in her voice.

Wharton whirled toward the sound, rifle still at the ready.

Rebecca shot him in the right shoulder, half an inch from the butt of the Springfield, which fired from the bolt. The .45-70 blasted loudly into the silence. The heavy slug passed close between Rebecca's shoulder and ear. The rifle clattered to the ground and Ben Wharton clutched at his shoulder. Wharton sank to his knees, his wife wailing beside him. She turned to help her wounded husband, eyes afire with hatred for Rebecca. A stirring in Jim Andrews's wagon took Rebecca's attention for the moment.

"I woulda stopped him if you didn't, Miss Rebecca," Damon Trent declared calmly from behind the tailgate. He held Toby's .32 Marlin to his shoulder.

"You never cease to amaze me, Damon," Rebecca gusted out in a sigh. Of a sudden, she realized she'd been holding her breath since her challenge to Wharton. "Get some help for Ben, please, someone."

"This don't change anything. We've sinned and sinned again," Alice Wharton shrieked. "The One will make us all pay."

Rebecca went to her, tried to comfort the distraught woman. "I'm sorry I had to shoot Ben, Mrs. Wharton . . . Alice. What you wanted to do would have left the rest of us to die."

"And you deserve it, too," Alice Wharton screamed. She started to raise the .32-20 Colt in her left hand, saw the revolver Rebecca held steady on her, and dropped the sixgun. In a wild gesture of desperation, Alice lashed out to claw at Rebecca's face. Rebecca easily caught the sharp-nailed hand and bent it harmlessly out of her way. Slowly she exerted pressure, forcing the enraged woman to her knees.

"There'll be no more of that. You came to us, remember? We had no obligation to bring you along. Your husband fought against the men of your sect, probably killed a few. There's nothing back there for you now. Your only hope . . . *our* only hope, is to survive this unfortunate setback and move onward to Yuma."

Some of the fury died in Alice's eyes and a tone of confused reason sounded when she spoke. "Wh-what about my Ben? You shot him."

"I did what had to be done. Didn't you hear Damon Trent? He had that Marlin carbine aimed at your husband. I'm not so certain he could place his bullet as carefully as I. Your actions precipitated it. Do you want your husband's death on your conscience, or on that of a small boy?"

Alice's face crumpled and she began to weep. Great sobs wracked her body while two men gently raised Ben Wharton to his feet and guided him to where his wound could be tended. A cumulative sigh rose from those gathered close.

"Well, we'd better finish making ready," Jim Andrews suggested. "This trail angled toward the Colorado River and the stage road, from what Lone Wolf told us before we left. If we aim in that general direction, southeast, we ought to find it. I'm for moving on now."

"No," Rebecca countered. "We should wait for a report from Lone Wolf and Joel."

Andrews shrugged. "Meanwhile, we and the stock get thirstier . . ."

"Can't be helped. I'll go check on Ben Wharton's wound," Rebecca concluded the subject.

Twenty minutes passed with the day growing warmer. Then a faint whoop sounded from beyond some featureless sand dunes. Hoofbeats thumped dully in the still desert, drawing nearer. A minute went by in tense expectation, then Lone Wolf crested the rise with Joel right behind, and forged down toward them.

"Good news," he called out before reining in. "We found the Colorado and the stage road. Two hours' travel from here on horseback. Four for the wagons. We can be there before the middle of the afternoon."

Chapter 23

Some comfort, Roger Styles grumbled to himself as he considered the Vallicito stage station. Dun-colored, made of adobe blocks, the Butterfield rest stop seemed less than a peasant's shack to a man accustomed to the luxury of the Crystal Palace. Worse, according to the driver, the hard part would begin in the morning, when the stagecoach would begin its laborious ascent into the Laguna Mountains. Another two days to San Diego. How could he possibly endure it?

"Mr. Styles," another passenger began. He eased himself onto the bench of a trestle table, opposite Roger, a mug of lukewarm beer in one hand. "You're in land development, as I understand it?"

"That's correct," Roger answered. He took in the rich quality of the stranger's clothing, the thick gold watch chain across his paunchy middle.

"Thinking of delving into San Diego properties?"

"It's a possibility," Roger hedged.

"Then I might be of help to you. Cleveland's the name. Marcus Cleveland. I'm an associate of Alonso

Horton. We need men of vision in San Diego. Alonso, quite confidentially, is near the end of his resources for further development. There's so many things to be done. So much land, waiting for the proper promotion. Perhaps we can interest you in having a part in that."

Roger contained his excitement while he gave back an expression of serious contemplation. "Ummm. Yes. You might indeed." Visions of millions swam in Roger's head. "May I call you Marcus?"

In a state of near-frenzy, the thirst-plagued survivors set out for the distant river. The word alone, *river*, held a promise of coolness and the opportunity to ease their burning bodies. Once atop the second rise from their overnight stay, the small column broke into a rapid trot. Jim Andrews felt a special urgency, the need to get the suffering boys to a place where they could immerse themselves in water. Jeeter Jenkins and Silas Miller willingly risked harm to their teams to hurry the distance away. A dozen mounted men raced ahead, tasked with the assignment of clearing the way.

Sand had drifted across the crude trail they followed. The outriders worked with shovels to remove the obstructions so the wagons could progress unhindered. The first mile of this work fell to those who remained with the slower-moving vehicles.

Alice Wharton, calmed down considerably, remained with her wounded husband in Jeeter Jenkins's wagon, second in line. A holiday mood seemed to infect most of the remaining people. Although still feverish and in terrible need of water, Toby Andrews and Damon Trent sat on the driver's seat of the Andrews' Conestoga and watched the monotonous scenery slowly slide past.

"May I have another swallow of water, Mr. Andrews?" Damon asked, his voice still a bit raspy.

With the prospect of replacement at hand, the tight restriction on consumption of potable water imposed by Joel Benchley and Rebecca Caldwell had been eased, though not yet done away with.

"Make it a small one," Jim Andrews informed the boy.

"Dad, it's funny," Toby piped up. "Here it is October, and it's hotter'n blazes on this desert."

Jim Andrews had to chuckle over this observation. "That's what makes it a desert, I suppose, Son. Another two hours and you can get right up to your ears in water. Over your head, if you want."

Excitement lighted both boys' eyes. Rebecca Caldwell turned her handsome Appaloosa and trotted back to the wagons. She gave the trio in the lead conveyance a cheerful wave.

"How are the boys doing, Jim?"

"Much better than I expected," Andrews replied with gratitude. "It's hard to believe we're so close to the river."

"I know what you mean," Rebecca agreed. "Śila's acting frisky already. It might take a bit longer than Lone Wolf implied, though."

"Why's that?"

"We'll have to make frequent stops to give a bit of water to the draft animals. I can sympathize with the desire for haste, but it's punishment for the mules."

Jim produced a rueful grin. "Not all that nice for people, either."

Rebecca nodded and sat in place until the next wagon came alongside. Then she began to trot her mount in time with the six-up driven by Jeeter Jenkins.

"I hope these critters make it," Jenkins grumbled. "In

this heat it's too fast, even with light loads."

"How's Ben Wharton?" Rebecca inquired.

"Hurtin', I reckon. Serves him right for what they tried."

"Don't be too hasty to judge. Long-time habits are hard to break."

"Beats me," Jenkins confided, "how you can be so tough one moment and soft as fresh-churned butter the next."

Rebecca favored him with a warm smile. "Perhaps it's because I'm a woman, Jeeter."

Jenkins flushed slightly. "*That*, I noticed."

Gradually, the pace slowed even more. Animals in desperate need of water moved ponderously, drawing their burdens with aching effort. Minutes crept into hours. The sun slanted well down the western sky when at last the final rise was topped. A ragged cheer came from the suffering travelers. Then, with the exception of Rebecca, Ian, and Joel, the mounted contingent raced their flagging horses down the sand slope toward the west bank of the Colorado River.

Misty-eyed, Rebecca blinked, her long black lashes moving in a delightful manner. "It's . . . so exciting. Yet, it's only a wide ribbon of rusty-colored water."

"And our salvation, I might add," Ian replied.

Lone Wolf rode out to greet them. He looked refreshed, and a big smile put a white slash in his sun-bronzed face. "That's terrible water," he admitted, "—though right now I don't think anyone will complain a great deal."

"We've made it," Rebecca enthused. Growing serious she admitted her inner, unrevealed fears. "There were times I believed we never would."

"There's a ford not far from here," Lone Wolf informed her. "A part of the stage road. We can cross

211

over and head due south to Yuma."

"If your destination is the California coast," Ian inquired, "why not stay on this side?"

"From here to the Mexican border, according to Joel," Rebecca told him, "there's only more of . . . this. Desert, cactus, and no water other than the river. We agreed everyone would want to rest up, remember? And you do need to seek new supplies."

Ian blushed slightly. "I, ah, must admit to having my geography a bit mixed up, until now. For some reason I believed we were on the east side of the river."

"It's a strange land to all of us," Lone Wolf offered to ease the minister's discomfort.

"Come on," Rebecca urged. "Let's go get wet."

Side by side, the wagons rolled to a stop a short distance from the other bank of the mighty river. Eagerly, people spilled from the vehicles to race toward the promise of relief. Jim Andrews rose from the seat to admonish his son and Damon Trent.

"I'll unhitch the mules and you take them with you," he advised.

"Awh, Dad . . . ?"

"They're the ones who got us here, Toby. Don't you think they deserve consideration?"

Toby shrugged. "Sure, Dad. We'll do it right away."

Most of the parched travelers flung themselves into the water fully clothed. Some of the men removed their shirts and sopped them, to squeeze out the accumulated moisture in rivulets that trickled over their sweaty torsos. Observing the universal rule of survival, the horses and mules received their refreshment first. The advent of their deliverance even affected Alice Wharton. In a quiet moment, following the initial rush, she sought out Rebecca Caldwell.

"Miss Caldwell, ah, Rebecca, I, er, what I want to

say is . . . I made a fool of myself and caused my husband to be hurt. I'm sorry for what we did. Can we make amends somehow?"

Rebecca reached out to take the shamefaced woman by both shoulders. "Of course we can. The pressures we were all under could cause any number of unfortunate incidents to happen. That you fell back on your former belief is not surprising. I think all of us did a lot of praying."

"I can see now how flawed Fat—uh, Fairgood Hollis was in his thinking. It's him I should blame for what happened to Ben."

"All in the past now. Come along, let's start filling water barrels."

The mules attended to, Toby and Damon put some distance between themselves and the joyous company. Around a slight bend, they quickly removed their clothing and leaped into the salving water. Shrill yelps of delight came from the youngsters as they splashed and cavorted. After a few minutes, they edged up to the bank and lay soaking in the reviving moisture.

"You know something?" Damon remarked after a long sigh of relief. "There's fish in here."

"Yeah. Lots of them."

"I bet we could catch a few."

"How? We don't have any line, hooks, or bait."

"We hog 'em out."

"What?"

"You've never done that? It's simple. Works better if you can *see* them, but it can be done. I got a big one nuzzling up to my side. All you have to do is slide your hand along their bodies, not too close so's to startle 'em. Then . . ."

Damon drew out the word as he moved swiftly, thrashed in the water, then grunted with effort and hauled a big five-pound catfish out of the ruddy depths. Unstable in the moving stream, it took him a moment to hurl his catch onto the bank.

"Simple. Like I told you. When you get your hand just right, you stick your thumb in your mouth and hook fingers in the gills. Then throw. You try it."

"It'll take a while. You scared the others away, I bet."

"We've got time, Toby," Damon assured him.

Back at the wagons, Ian finished watering animals and aiding with plugging the damaged barrels. He came to where Rebecca, Lone Wolf, and Joel conferred.

"Is there going to be time for me to go a bit south of here?"

"What for?" Joel asked bluntly.

"Thought I might bag some game. Fresh meat would be an added delight to all this water."

"We've been talking about time as it is," Rebecca informed him. "Joel and I think we shouldn't spend more than an hour here."

"Yep. It's a ways to the ford, accordin' to Lone Wolf, an' we want to get the wagons across before dark."

"Then perhaps I should hunt northward and catch up to you when you cross?"

"Good idea," Lone Wolf suggested. "A few rabbits or other game would savor the pot."

"What say I come along?" Rebecca inquired.

"I'd be delighted."

The pair departed, while the remainder of the caravan made ready to depart. Happy voices could be heard, bantering, in contrast to the solemn manner the morning began. Jim Andrews went in search of his son and Damon.

He returned, a huge grin on his face, with the two boys and three large catfish. "The boys caught them

214

with their bare hands," he exclaimed proudly.

"Rev'rand Claymore an' Rebecca have gone toward the ford huntin'," Joel informed him. "If they have any luck at all, we'll eat prime vittles tonight."

Once again, the wagons got on their way. The refreshed animals pulled with new energy. The ground had been packed hard by eons of time, baked by the sun. Travel proved easy. At the ford, Ian Claymore and Rebecca Caldwell waited with a bag of seven rabbits.

"Mighty fine shootin'," Joel expressed it for the entire company. "We'll get these wagons across with no trouble, I 'spect. If a stagecoach can do it, we can."

Red-brown water roiled around the ankles of the lead pair of Jim Andrews's mules. They snorted and stepped out at a lively pace. Rafe Baxter and another man preceded the wagon, boots off. They waded the ford, checking for any pitfalls.

"Someone's rocked it over at one time," Rafe Baxter called back.

"Right nice of them," Jim Andrews responded through a smile.

Without event, the Andrews wagon navigated the river and rolled onto the far bank. Jeeter Jenkins followed. His team shied a bit, then steadied into their task. Halfway across, and more than hub-deep, the wagon slewed to the side, creaking in protest.

Horsemen plunged into the water to fix ropes to the upstream side. From inside, cries of alarm came from the Wharton children.

"Steady, steady there," Jeeter called to his mules.

Straining into the harness, the six-up moved the wagon forward. When the water grew shallower, the team picked a faster pace. Jenkins spoke affectionately to his animals as they gained the far side. The last vehicle, driven by a grim-faced Silas Miller, made the traverse without incident.

"We ought to grease those axles," Jeeter suggested when the last rider had come over to the east side of the Colorado.

"We'll camp over that rise and do it then," Joel replied.

In a column once again, the train moved out toward the top of a low, rolling ridge. Rebecca, Lone Wolf and Ian crested it first.

They came face to face with a large, heavily armed party of silent, scowling Yuma Indians.

Chapter 24

Tension radiated like the sun-baked desert floor. For a long moment, no one spoke. Six more riders came beyond the ridge and halted, mouths sagging in dejection. To have come so far . . . Rebecca read the thought in their expressions.

"You *gringos*, you *viaje á* Yuma?" one squat, muscular Yuma inquired at last.

"To the city, ah, *el ciudad*," Ian Claymore responded. "*Comprende?*"

"*Ay, sí*. You go white-man town." His intelligent, shoe-button eyes took in the condition of the wagons. "You have trouble? *Combate, verdad?*"

"Yes, we had a fight. We, ah, certainly aren't looking for more."

The Yuma said something in his own language and the men with him smiled. "We no fight, *gringos*. You want, we go part way with you. Yuma *uno* day, *posiblé dos* that way."

Ian exchanged glances with Rebecca and Lone Wolf.

"Do we have any choice?" Rebecca asked practicably.

"Not that I can see," Ian admitted. He spoke again to the Yuma. "Thank you. *Gracias*. That would be nice of you."

"We hunt. Find food. *Por nuestros familias.*"

"Is your village far?" Rebecca asked.

"More days than to Yuma," came the answer. "I am called Teklah."

"I am Rebecca, this is Ian and our friend, Lone Wolf."

The spokesman for the Yumas looked critically at Rebecca and Lone Wolf. He tilted his head to one side and puckered his lips. At last he felt forced to ask the question.

"You dress different from other *gringos*. Why?"

"We prefer these clothes. Also, we both lived a long while with other people, Indians, far from here."

"Hummm. Is smart, but too much clothes for hot."

Such pleasantries ended with the arrival of the wagons. Rebecca made a short explanation and the abbreviated wagon train set off to the campsite location. The Yuma hunters walked alongside the wagons. Toby and Damon struck up a lively, if difficult, conversation with the one who understood some English. To the youngsters it represented yet another enjoyable adventure.

It took two and a half days to reach Yuma, Arizona Territory. The Yuma tribesmen departed from the travelers during the afternoon of the second day.

"Turned out to be swell fellers," Joel observed with relief. His opinion held for most.

Everyone's spirits picked up when the low buildings of Yuma appeared on the dust-hazed horizon to the south. At last they came to a stop in a large wagon yard next to the livery. Gratefully, the weary company set their feet on the ground in a genuine "civilized" community.

"What now?" Jim Andrews inquired.

"We'll have to find places to stay," Rebecca replied. "I, for one, will be thankful for a real bed."

General laughter followed and a voice called out, "We all will."

"Ian, I'll go on ahead and get you a room at the hotel, if you'd like to help Hester with her things."

"That's a bargain, Rebecca. Thank you."

"I'll walk along with you, if you don't mind, Rebecca," Jim Andrews offered. "We saw telegraph lines, and Damon's pestering me to get off a message to Dermott, Indiana, to inquire about his father."

Damon stood beside the tall, sandy-haired Andrews, his eyes alight with expectation. Next to him, Toby looked equally eager.

"And, of course, there's no way you can put it off until later," Rebecca answered lightly.

Andrews grinned. "Fact is, I'm sort of curious. If there's no word, or Damon's father has moved to elsewhere without leaving his destination . . . well, I wouldn't mind having two sons." He reached out and ruffled Damon's pale blond hair.

"And I'd have a brother," Toby piped up.

Together, they started off up the street. Not one to be hesitant, nor overly tactful, Toby asked an embarrassing question.

"Are you going to be staying on here with Reverend Claymore, Miss Rebecca?"

Rebecca flushed, her bronze cheeks darkening. "Why, ah, not exactly like that, Toby. Lone Wolf and I are going on to San Diego with the rest of you when you've rested up."

"Uh-huh. Only, I sorta thought, me an' Damon, that you might be, uh, gettin' married."

"Toby!" Jim Andrews blurted out. "What's come over you, Son?"

"Nothin', Dad," the youngster replied, head hanging.

"That was an impertinent question, young man."

"I'm sorry, Dad."

"You'll have to excuse him . . ." Jim began to Rebecca.

"No apology needed. And if there was, I'm sure Toby could manage his own."

"Whillikers, Miss Rebecca, I didn't mean to be nosy or anything. Just curiosity."

"Which has been said before to have killed the cat," his father reminded him.

Rebecca bent slightly, eyes fixed on Toby's. "This is for your information only, Toby. Ian and I like each other a great deal. But, he has his calling to the ministry, and I . . . I won't be satisfied until I bring Roger Styles and my uncle to justice. So, marriage is not in my immediate future. With Ian Claymore or anyone else."

A block further up the street, Rebecca paused. "Here's the hotel. I see a telegraph sign on down the way. So I'll say good-bye for now. It's been an adventurous trip, Jim."

"That it has."

"G'bye, Miss Rebecca," the boys chorused.

"Don't you two get into too much mischief," Rebecca cautioned. Smiling, she turned and entered the lobby.

Rebecca registered Ian and Hester for a room and got another for herself. Lone Wolf would stay in a loft over the livery, to keep an eye on their valuable Appaloosa horses. Satisfied with her accomplishment, though the clerk had given her travel-stained Sioux attire a critical look, she turned away from the desk, keys in her beaded pouch.

A heavy hand fell on her shoulder, causing Rebecca to turn swiftly.

She faced a large, beefy man, who wore the circled star of a United States marshal. "Are you Miss

Rebecca Caldwell?" he inquired.

"I am."

"I'm sorry, you'll have to come with me."

"Whatever for?"

"You're under arrest for suspicion of counterfeiting U.S. currency."

"Counterfeiting?"

Astonished, disbelieving, Rebecca had no choice but to accompany the lawman. How, she wondered, was she going to get out of this one . . .

BOLT

An Adult Western Series by Cort Martin

GREAT WESTERNS
by Dan Parkinson

THE SLANTED COLT   (1413, $2.25)
A tall, mysterious stranger named Kichener gave young
Benjamin Franklin Blake a gift. It was a gun, a colt pistol,
that had belonged to Ben's father. And when a cold-
blooded killer vowed to put Ben six feet under, it was a sure
thing that Ben would have to learn to use that gun — or die!

GUNPOWDER GLORY   (1448, $2.50)
Jeremy Burke, breaking a deathbed promise to his pa,
killed the lowdown Sutton boy who was the cause of his
pa's death. But when the bullets started flying, he found
there was more at stake than his own life as innocent
people were caught in the crossfire of *Gunpowder Glory.*

BLOOD ARROW   (1549, $2.50)
Randall Kerry returned to his camp to find his companion
slaughtered and scalped. With a war cry as wild as the savages', the young scout raced forward with his pistol held
high to meet them in battle.

BROTHER WOLF   (1728, $2.95)
Only two men could help Lattimer run down the sheriff's
killers — a stranger named Stillwell and an Apache who was
as deadly with a Colt as he was with a knife. One of them
would see justice done — from the muzzle of a six-gun.

CALAMITY TRAIL   (1663, $2.95)
Charles Henry Clayton fled to the west to make his fortune, get married and settle down to a peaceful life. But
the situation demanded that he strap on a six-gun and ride
toward a showdown of gunpowder and blood that would
send him galloping off to either death or glory on the . . .
Calamity Trail.

TALES OF THE OLD WEST

SPIRIT WARRIOR   (1795, $2.50)
by G. Clifton Wisler
The only settler to survive the savage indian attack was a little boy. Although raised as a red man, every man was his enemy when the two worlds clashed—but he vowed no man would be his equal.

IRON HEART   (1736, $2.25)
by Walt Denver
Orphaned by an indian raid, Ben vowed he'd never rest until he'd brought death to the Arapahoes. And it wasn't long before they came to fear the rider of vengeance they called . . . Iron Heart.

WEST OF THE CIMARRON   (1681, $2.50)
by G. Clifton Wisler
Eric didn't have a chance revenging his father's death against the Dunstan gang until a stranger with a fast draw and a dark past arrived from West of the Cimarron.

HIGH LINE RIDER   (1615, $2.50)
by William A. Lucky
In Guffey Creek, you either lived by the rules made by Judge Breen and his hired guns—or you didn't live at all. So when Holly took sides against the Judge, it looked like there would be just one more body for the buzzards. But this time they were wrong.

GUNSIGHT LODE   (1497, $2.25)
by Virgil Hart
When Ned Coffee cornered Glass and Corey in a mine shaft, the last thing Glass expected was for the kid to make a play for the gold. And in a blazing three-way shootout, both Corey and Coffee would discover how lightening quick Glass was with a gun.

Available wherever paperbacks are sold, or order direct from the Publisher. Send cover price plus 50¢ per copy for mailing and handling to Zebra Books, Dept. 1882, 475 Park Avenue South, New York, N.Y. 10016. Residents of New York, New Jersey and Pennsylvania must include sales tax. DO NOT SEND CASH.